Lauren Ipsum

BEGIN
1
MILE
0

Typeset in Sorts Mill Goudy with X∃TEX.

ISBN-13 978-1-461178187

ISBN-10 1-461178185

Open Library OL24973821M

Zeroth English Edition, December 2011

The Computers in this Book

I feel I should warn you. No computers will be found in this book. If the idea of a computer science book without computers upsets you, please close your eyes until you've finished reading the rest of this page.

The truth is that computer science is not really about the computer. It is just a tool to help you see ideas more clearly. You can see the moon and stars without a telescope, smell the flowers without a fluoroscope, have fun without a funoscope, and be silly sans oscilloscope.

You can also play with computer science without you-know-what. Ideas are the real stuff of computer science. This book is about those ideas, and how to find them.

Mostly Lost

Lauren Ipsum had been lost in the woods all morning. The poor girl didn't know where she was or where she was going.

It all started with an argument. Her mother wanted her to go to summer school, and naturally Laurie didn't. Children in Finland go to school year round, her mom said. They weren't in Finland, Laurie said. Extra classes are how to get ahead, mom said. Summer is for having fun, Laurie said. The argument went on and on and got loud near the end. To calm down Laurie took a walk in the woods.

When people are faced with something they don't want to do, they often do something else they aren't allowed to do. Before long Laurie had gone farther into the woods than she had ever gone before.

Being lost was kind of fun. Out here Laurie could be anything she wanted to be and there was no one to tell her different.

She was a secret ninja, moving like a ghost through the ancient forest. Light and shadow danced under the leaves, and she danced with them. No one could hear her stealthy ninja footsteps. No one would see her coming until it was too—

"*Chiguire!*" said a voice up ahead. A shape came toward her out of the darkness. Was it an angry spirit? A dire beast?

"*Argot!*" it said. It was like a mouse-dog, or a dog-mouse. That is to say, it was a creature the size of a dog but looking like a mouse. It walked right up to her and began nuzzling her hand in a very un-beast-like way.

"Aw, you're so friendly!" Laurie said, in what was a rather un-ninja-like fashion.

"*Repl!*" it said, and put a webbed foot on her knee.

"You're a funny-looking thing, aren't you? What's your name, huh? What should I call you?"

"*Argot!*"

"Ok, I'll call you Argot. Are you hungry? What do... things like you eat?" She offered it some peanuts.

"*Snarfl!*" it snarfled, eating out of her hand.

"Hey little guy," she said, tickling its chin, "you don't know the way back to Hamilton, do you?"

"*Hamilton!*" it said excitedly.

"You do know a way?"

"*Lalr!*" it lalred, tongue hanging out.

"So where is it?"

"*Isit!*" it said.

"I mean, how do I get there?"

"*Gether!*" it said.

"You're just repeating what I'm saying, aren't you?"

"*Arentyou!*" it said.

"That's what I thought. Animals can't talk."

So now I'm lost, Laurie thought to herself. *How do I get unlost?* She remembered something about moss growing on the north side of trees. There wasn't any moss, so that was out. *The sun rises in the east and sets in the west.* It was late morning and the sun was almost overhead. No help there either.

She wandered around, flipping her lucky red poker chip. If the chip landed on Heads, she walked to the left for a while. If it landed on Tails, she walked to the right for a while.

"*Burble...*" Argot waddled behind her, making nonsense noises.

"No, don't follow me, Argot. Shoo!"

"*Bitblit?*"

"I like you, but I'm not allowed to have a dog. Or a mouse, or a dog-mouse, or whatever you are. Go along now, go home!"

No matter what she said, the ugly little thing wouldn't give up. It seemed willing to follow Laurie all the way to... wherever she was going.

Maybe if I wait for the stars to come out, she thought to herself. *No, that's silly. I don't know which stars are which!*

"*Frobit!*" Another creature like Argot, but bigger, came out of the underbrush. It tried to lick her face.

"Ugh, your breath stinks!"

"*Wibble!*" A third creature came up from behind and butted its head against her.

"Whoops! Hello to you, too."

"*Tanstaafl!*"

"*Zork!*"

More creatures were coming from all directions. The noise was getting louder.

"Uh," Laurie uhhed.

"*Parsec!*"

"*Wurfl!*"

"*Lilo!*"

Argot's friends were no longer just nuzzling. They were crowding all around her, pushing and shouting. She was being mobbed.

Laurie panicked and ran. The gang of creatures howled and chased after her.

"*Nyquist!*"

"*Quux!*"

"*Fifo!*"

She could barely stay on her feet, running through the tangled underbrush, but she was too afraid to slow down.

Her escape was blocked by a tall green hedge that stretched off in both directions. Once upon a time it might have been part of a garden, but now it was wild and disorderly. Laurie squeezed her way through a gap in the hedge and kept running until she thought she was safe. The creatures were far behind.

The forest looked different on the other side of the hedge. For one, the trees had red and black stripes. Black tree trunks split into two red branches. Those split into four black branches, which split into eight red branches, and on and on, until the branches ended in millions of tiny black leaves. In fact...

"*Foo!*"

"*Bar!*"

"*Baz!*"

The creatures were still chasing her! Laurie tried to run away again but she couldn't go very fast. Her throat was raw and her legs were almost numb.

"Help! Stop it!" she cried. "Make them stop!"

"*Wysiwyg!*"

A small man carrying a large pack stepped in between her and the mob. Dishes and pots and pans and cowbells rattled around. The creatures halted a few paces away, making awful angry noises.

"Are you OK, miss?" he said.

"These— these *mouse dogs* won't leave me alone!"

"*Epsilon!*"

"*Olap!*"

"It's just a bunch of Jargon," he said. "Hold still and stay calm." He cupped his hands to his mouth.

"STANI!" he shouted at them.

All of the Jargon froze, their ears aquiver.

"CEPAT! AFVIGE! *SCHNELL! SCHNELL!*"

And just like that, they were gone.

Laurie collapsed against a tree. "Th-thank you," she said.

"Sure thing, miss. Just rest here a while," the man said. He dropped his pack with a loud jangle, then sat on top of it.

"What's a Jargon?" she asked once she'd caught her breath.

"Jargon live in the swamps. They feed on attention. If they can't get that, they'll settle for fear and confusion."

"But the first one was so friendly! I just talked to it a little and it started following me."

"That's how it starts," he said. "A little Jargon doesn't look like much. Some people even keep them as pets. But they form packs, and they are very dangerous."

"That's terrible!"

He shrugged. "What can you do? Stand your ground and act confident. If you show any fear, a pack of wild Jargon will run you right over."

"What did you say to make them leave?"

"I have no idea. It sounded good, though, didn't it?" he said. "So what's your name, miss?"

"My name is Laurie. I think I'm lost."

"That's wonderful!" the man said. "I'm lost too."

"Oh no! You mean you don't know where you are?"

"No, I know exactly where I am."

"So you don't know where you're going?"

"I know exactly where I'm going. I'm on the way home."

Laurie was almost too confused to feel confused. "But if you know where you *are*," she said, "and you know where you're *going*, how can you be lost?"

"Because I don't know how I'll get there," the man grinned. "I'm a Wandering Salesman."

"A Wandering Salesman? What's that?"

"We wander from town to town, selling and buying. There are two rules: You have to visit every town before going home, and you can't visit any town twice. Every road is the road home except the road behind me."

"So you always go to the next place you've never been to?" she asked.

"That's right! You're guaranteed to get home eventually," he said. "It's only logical. Along the way I've seen the sunrise over the Towers of Hanoi and climbed the Upper Bounds. I've sat down at the Lookup Table and floated on the Overflow River. It's a good life. Being lost can be fun!"

"It's not fun for me anymore," said Laurie. "I don't really know where I am, or where I'm going, *or* how to get there."

"Hmm. Mostly lost is fun, but completely lost is serious. You are going home too, right?"

"Yes, I want to go home!" she said.

"And where do you live?"

"I live in Hamilton with my mom. Do you know where it is?"

"Not a clue. Never heard of it!" he said cheerfully. "But that's one out of three, anyway. You have a definite goal."

"Um, I guess so."

"And I know where *I* am, and since we're in the same place, that means I know where *you* are. You are in the Red-Black Forest, near Mile Zero."

The what near who? she thought to herself, but the man was still talking.

"...now you know where you are and where you are going!" the Salesman said. "You are only *mostly* lost."

"But I still don't know how to get there!"

"Hmm," he hmmed, thinking it over. "I know someone you should talk to: a wise lady named Eponymous Bach."

"Where is she?"

"She lives in Bach Haus at the end of Bach Way, in the town of—"

"Bach?"

"How did you guess? Bach is an excellent Composer. At the very least she can name your problem."

That sounded like a much better plan than watching moss grow!

"OK, I'll do it. Will you go with me?"

"I would love to, Laurie. But I've just come from visiting Bach," said the Salesman.

"Oh. That means you can't go back, right?"

"Right. I can take you up to the road, but from there you are on your own."

The Wandering Salesman showed her the way to the edge of the forest. Just past the last tree was a road sign. "Ah, here we are," he said. "Route One, Mile Zero."

"I've never seen a Mile ZERO," said Laurie.

"Everything has to start somewhere. It may not look like much, but this is a very special place. You might even say it's the starting point of the whole System."

"What comes after Mile Zero?"

"Mile One, of course. And right after that is the town of Bach. Are you ready?"

"Yes, I think so. Thank you!"

"You're welcome, Laurie. Good luck! Maybe our paths will cross again." The Wandering Salesman headed off, cowbells and pans rattling, to a place he'd never been before.

And so did Laurie.

A Hidden Ally

"That wasn't *too* bad," Laurie said to herself, as she reached the Mile One sign. "A mile sounds like a long way to walk, but it's only eight blocks."

"*Oh look, another one.*" said a voice.

"Hello?" Laurie spun around, but there wasn't much to see: some odd-looking crops, an empty road, and the sign.

"*She's kind of short, isn't she?*"

That's when she noticed a tiny lizard clinging to the sign. It had the oddest coloring: where the sign was green, the lizard was reddish; where it was white, the lizard was black.

"Hello, what are you?" she asked.

"I'm Xor," the lizard squeaked. His tail twitched from yellow to blue. "Hold on, can you *see* me?"

"Of course I can see you!" Laurie said.

"Oh." Xor looked very sad and blushed a bright purple.

"You *are* the first talking lizard I've ever met," Laurie said. "How did you learn to talk?"

"What a silly question!" the creature said. "I learned as a baby, like everybody."

"You did?"

"Sure. Why, how did *you* learn to talk?"

"Well..." She had always been able to talk, hadn't she? "I guess I learned as a baby too."

"It's only logical. First you learn to talk, then you learn to think. Too bad it's not the other way round."

"What are you doing there on the sign?" Laurie asked.

"Another silly question! What does it look like I'm doing? I am blending into the background," Xor said. At that moment he turned pink and violet. "Did you say something?"

She shook her head.

"Where was I? Oh yes. Blending in is an honorable and ancient art. It takes years of practice. You must have a pretty sharp eye to spot me." Xor marched around the sign as he talked, turning white with large orange polka-dots.

Laurie bit her tongue, trying not to laugh.

"No, you don't see a lizard like me every day!" He turned peach and cornflower blue. "But sometimes —personally speaking between you and me, of course— sometimes..." he looked sad again and fell silent.

"Sometimes what?"

"Sometimes, I worry I'm not doing it right."

"Not if you want to *hide*!" Laurie said, unable to contain herself. "Your colors keep changing."

"I was pretty sure I'd figured it out this time," Xor said, turning his head around to get a better look at himself. "My left leg is green–"

"Green? No, it's red."

"Really?"

"Really. Now it's purple."

Xor sighed. "Blending in is a lot harder than it looks. I'm glad it was you who saw me and not a hungry bird. You see, I'm a bit color-blind."

"What kind of lizard are you anyway?" she asked.

"I'm Chameleon, mostly. I'm part dinosaur on my mother's side."

"Part *dinosaur*? That's impossible."

"It's true!" Xor drew his little self up proudly. "For instance, my great-aunt Vana is a Steganosaurus. She can hide anywhere, even on the back of a postage stamp."

Laurie wasn't sure she believed Xor, but she didn't want to hurt the lizard's feelings.

"Maybe your aunt can teach you how to hide better."

"I'd love that. But I don't know where she is. The last time I saw her, I didn't even see her!" he said.

"But—"

"*Hey*," Xor said, "why don't I come along with *you*? If you can see me, maybe you'll be able to see her, too."

"I don't think—"

"It'll be fine! I know a lot about this place. I can show you around."

"Well, I can carry you in my pocket," Laurie said. "Have you heard of Hamilton?"

"I don't know. Can you eat it?"

"Never mind. Let's go."

Sense & Sensibleness

They soon reached the little town of Bach. It was very confusing at first, because the name "Bach" appeared on everything: Bach Street, Bach Avenue, Bach Plaza, even the sidewalk was called the sidebach. They finally found Bach Haus down the Bach Way.

Laurie knocked on the great door. A tall lady in an elegant coat and frizzy white hair answered. "Hello, what can I do for you?" she asked.

"Are you Eponymous Bach? I was told you can help me."

"If I can't help solve your problem, I can at least give it a name. Do come in and have some tea."

The house was impressive on the outside, but on the inside it was a mess! Strange machines were shoved against the walls, cobwebs hung down from the corners, tools were scattered on the floor, and piles and piles of paper with scribbled notes were everywhere. A violin was stuffed into a flower pot. Xor jumped out of Laurie's pocket to hunt some insects.

"Um, so you are a composer?"

"That's right," said Eponymous.

"What kind of music do you compose?"

"Oh, I don't compose music," she said. "I compose Ideas!"

"You compose... ideas? How?"

"I put little ideas together to make bigger ones. Then I put those ideas together to make even bigger and bigger ones! And then I put my name on them. You shouldn't let any ideas escape without a name," she said. "That's Bach's First Law of Eponymy. I made it myself, you see."

"Is that why all the streets are named after you?" Laurie asked.

"Yes, I used to put my name on Things. But it's much better to have your name on an Idea. That's my Second Law of Eponymy."

"But why is an idea better?" Laurie asked. "You can't see an idea."

"Because good ideas never wear out! You put your name on a birthday cake, but it doesn't last very long, does it?"

"No. You eat it right away." Laurie said. Birthday cakes don't last long at all!

"You can also put your name on a mountain," said Eponymous. "But even mountains fall down eventually. It makes a terrible noise, too! No, the best way to make something last forever is to take away everything but the ideas." She pointed to a portrait of a man with curly hair and a funny coat.

"That is my friend Andy Ampere. One day, he noticed that when he put electricity through two wires, they would bend a little toward each other. So he called it Andy's Magical Wire Bender, and he went around selling it to people who make paper clips."

"That's pretty neat!"

"Yes, but I told Andy to keep going, to take away all of the Things until he had an Idea worth putting his name on. He realized he could use his machine to measure electricity by looking at how much the wires bent. That was truly new; a new law of nature. Nobody uses Andy's Magical Wire Bender anymore, but Ampere's Law will always be current."

"But why do you put your name on everything?"

"Names are very important! A thing without a name is like a pot without a handle. Just try telling a story about turtles without using the word 'turtle'."

"Well," said Laurie, always ready to argue a point, "you could say 'a Green Round animal with a Shell' instead of 'turtle'."

"Hrmph," Eponymous hrmphed, "That's not a very easy name, but I suppose it will do. So how can I help you, child?"

"I'm looking for a path back to Hamilton. The Wandering Salesman said I just have to go everywhere I've never been before, and eventually I'll find my way home. But..."

"But what, dear?"

"I don't know, something about what he said doesn't make sense."

"It might make SENSE, but it may not be SENSIBLE," said Eponymous.

"Isn't that the same thing?" asked Laurie.

"Many things make sense but are not sensible at all! You can go from the front door to the back door by walking through the house, right?"

"Sure."

"You can also walk round the outside of the house, or even all the way round the planet to do the same thing. Many ways make sense, but only some are sensible."

"Then I want to find a sensible way," said Laurie. "I don't want to walk all round the planet!"

"So," Eponymous said, "we have named and framed your problem: Laurie's Quest is to find the shortest path home."

"But how do I do that?" asked Laurie. "Is it difficult?"

"You'll never know unless you try. The next town up the road is called Symbol. Have you been there before?"

"No, I've never even heard of it."

"Then it sounds perfect. Just follow Bach Avenue out of town, and take a left at Recursion Junction."

"That's great!" said Laurie. "Xor, let's go. Oh, that's right," she remembered. "Do you know anything about how to find Steganosauruses?"

Eponymous smiled. "Who's been telling you stories like that, my dear girl? Steganosauruses don't exist."

Rounding Error

As they headed out of Bach, Laurie couldn't help but tease Xor a little. "Steganosauruses don't exist, huh?"

"That lady doesn't know what she's talking about. Her place had some really good bugs, though."

"Maybe she's right."

"She says they don't exist because she's never seen one. But that proves my point. Steganosauruses are so good at hiding that people think they are imaginary."

"That doesn't make any sense, Xor."

"Who are you going to believe, me or your own eyes?"

Squawk! Laurie felt something brush her shoulder. Before she knew it a fat bird was flying away with Xor in its talons.

"Hey!" She ran after as it slowly flew to a nearby branch. The bird was so fat it was almost spherical, the size and shape of a coconut. There were two more just like it in the tree.

She jumped at the bird holding Xor, but it tossed the lizard to another bird who caught him in its beak. She jumped at that one but Xor was thrown to another.

The birds enjoyed playing keep-away. When their mouths weren't full of lizard they hopped up and down and sang a silly rhyme:

"Faster and faster—"
"—too fast to follow—"
"—Round Robins throw faster—"
"—than an unladen swallow!"

"Give him back!" Laurie shouted. "He's my friend!" The Round Robins only cackled and mocked her.

"Give him back!"

  "Give him back!"

    "We think he will make—"

      "—an afternoon snack!"

"Help!" Xor squeaked in terror. "They want to eat me!"

"Thought he was hiding—"

  "—but bird eyes can see—"

    "—an evenly dividing—"

      "—meal for three!"

"No!" Laurie picked up a stone and threw it at the nearest Round Robin. To her utter surprise it didn't fly away. The fat nasty thing *caught the stone.*

"A stone!"

  "How rude!"

    "Hardly a treasure."

"We'll happily juggle it—"
"—for your pleasure!"

They played catch with the stone and Xor. She threw another and another, and the birds caught them too. Now the Round Robins were juggling three stones plus Xor. This wasn't going anywhere. Laurie paused, thinking, another stone in her hand.

"Gave up so soon?"
"We love to play ball!"
"Throw us more toys—"
"—and we'll catch them all!"

Instead of throwing the stone she scooped up a large handful and started tossing them in nice easy lobs, one by one. The Robins caught each one and juggled it. If they hadn't been trying to eat her friend, Laurie would have been impressed.

"What are you doing? Save me!" Xor said.

Soon the three Robins were having trouble keeping them all in the air. Laurie threw the stones harder and faster, trying to put them off balance. They sang for reinforcements.

"More wings, my brothers!"
"More beaks and more talons!"
"We need more Round Robins—"
"—to evenly balance!"

Five more of the creatures flapped and flopped in to join the party of their murderous kin. They evened out the load of stones and mocked her even louder.

"You can't beat us that way!"
    "We'll have our meal!"
        "Each one will eat less—"
            "—but a deal's a deal!"

Fifteen, twenty, twenty-five stones now. They could catch whatever she threw at them. A dozen more of the creatures were waiting to join in. How could she get Xor away from them?

"Clever Round Robins,"
    "too many to beat!"
        "You can't stop the Robins—"
            "—when there's dinner to eat!"

It was hard to concentrate with the birds singing and Xor screaming, but Laurie waited again, trying to see a pattern. A Round Robin can catch anything...

"Round he goes!"
    "Where will he stop?"
        "Stones all a-juggle,"
            "but the lizard won't—*mmph!*"

Just as one of the birds was about to catch Xor, Laurie hit him in the beak with a nice big clod of dirt. A Round Robin can catch anything. But not *two* things.

She caught Xor as he fell and ran away as fast as she could. Stones and furious Robins flew everywhere as the flock lost its rhythm. Some tried to chase her but they were too fat to keep up and too angry to rhyme.

"No fair!"

"No fair!"

"You stole our snack!"

"Come back!"

"No fair!"

"You stole..."

"Are you OK?" Laurie said.

"No... Yes... Maybe." Xor was breathing hard. They both were. He didn't look hurt, but the little lizard was scared out of his wits. "Birds."

"This is why you have to blend in, isn't it?" she asked. "Birds want to eat you."

"I hate birds."

What the Tortoise Said to Laurie

Laurie took a left turn at the sign marked "Recursion Junction". After cresting a little hill she ended up at... Recursion Junction!

"Is this the same place, Xor?" Laurie asked. "It looks the same."

"Try a right turn," he said.

She did, but after a short while they were back where they started. When she tried a second, and a third, and twenty-seventh time, they always came back to Recursion Junction.

"It seems as though I am going somewhere else, but we always come back to the same place. What's going on?"

They went round

    ...and round

        ...and round

            ...and round so many times that Laurie lost count. Just as she was about to give up, the next turn round put her on a different road.

This road was neat and straight, and seemed to stretch on forever. A man in a Greek helmet was sitting on a large, Round, Green animal with a Shell. They were moving slowly and steadily away.

"Hey! Wait!" Laurie shouted, running up to the pair.

"At last, someone has caught up to us!" said the animal.

"I thought that was IMPOSSIBLE," said the man.

"Hello!" the animal said to Laurie. "I am Tortoise, a humble tortoise." He was much too large to be a mere *turtle*. "This is my esteemed companion, Achilles the Logician."

"At your service, miss!" said Achilles, bowing to her from his perch atop Tortoise.

"Um, Hello. My name is Lauren Ipsum." She attempted a curtsey.

"How did you get here, Miss Ipsum?" asked Tortoise.

"I don't really know," Laurie said. "We were following the path to Symbol but I got turned around at Recursion Junction."

"That often happens. You spent quite a bit of time chasing your tail, I imagine."

"I don't have a tail," she said.

"So it got away from you, did it?"

"What? I don't—"

"Perhaps it was optimized away," said Tortoise. "No matter. Most of you made it through, and that's the important thing. You can help us resolve a question."

"Well, I can try." Laurie said, not sure that she and Tortoise were having the same conversation.

"Splendid!" said Tortoise. "The question my dear friend Achilles and I are considering is this: How long is an infinite piece of string?"

"An infinite string? Infinite means it's really really really really really REALLY long. Really." said Laurie. Really.

"So you agree with ME," Achilles said. "That means the burden of proof must be borne by the other side."

"The burden of Achilles on my BACK is more than enough!" the Tortoise grumbled.

"Friend Tortoise is wise about many things," said Achilles. "But he is clearly wrong this time. He says that an infinite string can be exactly TWO INCHES long!"

"But how can an infinite string be two inches long?" Laurie asked.

"His claim is preposterous and indiscrete," said Achilles. "We are in continuous disagreement."

"I never disagree," said Tortoise. "I only discuss, especially with an intellect such as yours, Achilles. Your understanding has no limit."

"You are too kind, dear Tortoise."

"I mean every word," said Tortoise. "Allow me to suggest a way to settle the question by Experiment."

"Please, suggest away," said Achilles.

"Let us build —hypothetically, of course!— an infinitely long piece of string, and then measure it. Miss Ipsum can be our impartial judge."

"I accept. Experiment is always better than mere Theory," Achilles said. "And an impartial judge sounds wonderful, especially when she already agrees with me!"

"Excellent," said Tortoise. "Miss Ipsum, imagine you have an infinite number of little pieces of string. If you laid them all end-to-end, would that be infinitely long? Hypothetically?"

"Yes, it must be." said Laurie.

"Infinity is infinity," said Achilles. "It's only logical."

"I wonder. Suppose we start with a piece of string ONE inch long," Tortoise said. "Then add a second piece of string that is ONE-HALF inch long. How long are they together?"

"One-and-a-half inches," Laurie said.

"And that is shorter than two inches?" Tortoise asked.

"One-half inch shorter. Unmistakably." Achilles said.

"We all agree thus far," said Tortoise. "Perhaps we shall converge upon the same conclusion."

"I doubt that!" said Achilles. Laurie wasn't sure what Tortoise was getting at, but she doubted too.

"Achilles, would you please keep count of our hypothetical string? I want to add a third piece ONE-QUARTER of an inch long," said Tortoise. "Is our string now one-and-three-quarters inches long?"

Achilles retrieved a much-used notebook from under his helmet and scribbled some figures. "It seems so," he said.

"With one-quarter inch to spare?" asked Tortoise.

Scribble. "Yes, only one-quarter inch! You are a finger's-width away from defeat!"

"Add an EIGHTH-inch piece," Tortoise said. "Do I still have some space left over?"

"Yes, but I'll have beaten you soon!" the Greek Logician crowed. "Your string is an eighth-inch away from the limit, and you've only done FOUR pieces!"

"Your arithmetic is correct as always, Achilles. But in the interest of science, let us continue until the bitter end," Tortoise said.

"It won't be long," said Achilles. "What is your next move?"

"I would like to add another piece of string, this time one-sixteenth inch long."

"Done!" Scribble. "Only one-sixteenth inch left, old friend!"

"Only that much?" said Tortoise. "Then for the next one, I would like to add a piece of string one-thirty-second inch long."

"As you wish, poor Tortoise. One-thirty-second of an inch. There is only one-thirty-second inch remaining, and an infinity of strings to go! There will be PLENTY of rope left over to hang yourself with!" said Achilles.

"Please add a sixty-fourth inch piece," said Tortoise, "then a one-hundred-twenty-eighth inch piece, and a two-hundred-and-fifty-sixth inch piece, and then a five-hundred-twelveth inch piece of string, and then—"

"Slow down, Tortoise! You are going too fast," Achilles said. "And those are very big— no, very SMALL numbers." He figured and scribbled for a minute. "There is only a five-hundred-and-twelveth inch remaining. It's too bad we're not splitting HAIRS, or you could have gotten a little farther! Do you give up now?"

"*Oh.* I see!" exclaimed Laurie. "Achilles, Tortoise is right."

"What? Don't change your mind NOW when we are so close to victory!" Achilles cried.

"No, I'm sure Tortoise is right," said Laurie. "Don't you see? Every piece he adds is HALF as long as the one before. That leaves just enough room left over. Even if he adds an infinite number of pieces, it will NEVER reach two inches."

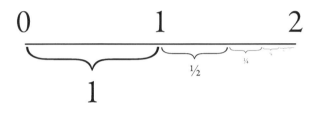

"Well, hardly ever," said Tortoise.

Achilles grimaced. "It appears you've proven the impossible again, Tortoise. But just to make sure, I will check the arithmetic MYSELF." He continued to scribble in his notebook:

+ 1/512 inch
  + 1/1,024 inch
    + 1/2,048 inch
      + 1/4,096 inch
        + 1/8,192 inch
          + 1/16,384 inch
            + 1/32,768 inch
              + 1/65,536 inch
                + 1/131,072 inch
                  + 1/262,144 inch...

"THAT should keep him busy. Thank you for your assistance, Miss Ipsum."

"You're welcome, Mister Tortoise," said Laurie. "I didn't know something so big could be so small."

"That's the Power of Two," said Tortoise. "If you cut a number into two halves, then cut it in two again, and so on, very soon it will be too small to see. But there will always be something left over."

"Mister Tortoise, do you know how long this road is? It feels like it goes on forever. I'm trying to get to Symbol."

"This road is quite long," said Tortoise. "In fact, it is infinite."

"Oh, no! How do I get to the end?"

"That can be done in two simple steps."

"How?"

"How do you think? A step with your right foot, then a step with your left foot. Your point of view is what's important. It's integral."

Laurie closed her eyes and took a deep breath. When she opened her eyes, Achilles and Tortoise were gone. The infinite road was a tiny short thing now, hardly a sidewalk. She stepped forward with her right foot. Then she stepped again with her left foot. In front of her was a road sign that said...

Welcome to Symbol

The town of Symbol was surrounded by high and perfectly smooth walls. A large stream split into two and flowed around either side of the town.

"Do you know anything about this place?" Laurie asked.

"The people are kind of strange," said Xor.

"What does that mean?"

"You'll see."

The path led to a gateway with a turnstile. It looked like this: $\models$

Two boys about her age were serving as guards. One wore a bright white suit and a black shirt. The other had a bright black suit and a white shirt.

Maybe they'll ask me a riddle, Laurie thought. *Or I'll need to figure out which one is a liar and which one tells the truth!* Laurie had read a lot of fairytale books, you see. She believed she was learning how this place worked.

"Name?" asked one.

"Laurie Ipsum."

"Password?" asked the other.

"Why, I don't know the password," Laurie said.

"Then you may not enter!" the boys said in unison.

"That's not much of a riddle."

"A riddle? Ha ha, no, begging your pardon, miss. That's not how it works. There are no riddles, no bets, no liars, or truth-tellers. We've read those books, haven't we, Tollens?"

33

"Yes we have, Ponens. There's none of that mythic fairybook stuff in our System, miss. Word games and clever riddles, ha! That's just bad security!"

"But that's not fair! How do I get inside?"

"It's very simple," said Ponens. "If you have a password, that means you can pass through the semantic turnstile."

"If you can't pass through the turnstile, that means you don't have a password. It's only logical." Tollens said.

"Do you have a password?" Ponens asked.

"No, I don't know what it is," she said.

"Then you may not enter!" They said again, together.

"Can you give me a hint?"

"Yes, hints are part of the System," said Ponens.

"Oh, good."

"Did you set up a hint with your account?"

"Well, no," she said. "This is my first time here."

"Then it's hard luck for you, miss," said Tollens. "Once you are inside, do make sure to set up a hint for the next time."

"...and remember to change your password to something memorable, but hard to guess," said Ponens. "It's just good security."

"But I'm trying to *get* inside! I don't know what to do!"

"It's very simple," said Ponens. "If you have a password, that means you can pass through the semantic turnstile."

"And if you can't pass through the turnstile, that means you don't have a password. It's only logical," Tollens said.

"That's not completely true, is it?" Laurie said. "What if the turnstile is broken? I wouldn't be able to enter even if I had a password."

"Um," Tollens ummed, looking a little unsure of himself.

"Or what if I fooled you into *believing* I had the password, even if I didn't? Then I could enter without it."

"Hmm," Ponens hmmed, trying to find a flaw in her argument.

Laurie rushed on. "Or what if I had the password, but I didn't want to give it to you?"

"No, you still couldn't encroach on our premises," Ponens said with more confidence. "You have to give us a password that matches the name you gave us."

"Is it 'Laurie'?" she guessed.

"No!" they shouted together.

"Is it 'November First'?" for that was Laurie's birthday.

"No!" they shouted again.

"Only one try left, miss," said Tollens.

"Oh, no! Really?"

"You can try only so many times. It's just good security."

"Do I even have an account?" she wondered.

"We can't confirm or deny that," answered Ponens. "That would be bad security."

"Do I *not* have an account?"

"We can't deny or confirm that either!" answered Tollens.

"It's very simple—" began Ponens.

"—yes, yes," Laurie interrupted. "If I have it, I know it, but if I don't you can't tell me, and you can give me a hint only if I set it up earlier!" This certainly was very good security! *Think, Laurie, think!*

"OK. Let's start over," she said.

"Very well, miss," said Tollens. "Name?"

"I told you, it's Lau—" she stopped herself. "Actually... my name is Eponymous Bach."

"Password?" said Ponens.

It couldn't be that simple, could it?

"Bach's Password."

"Welcome!" said Ponens and Tollens, waving her through the turnstile.

Of course Bach would name her password after herself!

A Tinker's Trade

When they were safely inside the town walls, the little lizard popped his head out of Laurie's pocket.

"See what I mean? Let's hope they don't figure out what you did to get in here," Xor said. "So, why are we here?"

"We're looking for information. Maybe we can find a map or something."

"Oh," said Xor. "I was hoping you were going to say food. Why don't we try this place?"

In front of them was a storefront with a very fancy sign painted on the window:

N. Veterate Tinker
Algorithms & Abstractions
BUY * SELL * TRADE

"Al-go-rith-ms. That sounds like a kind of fruit."

"Are you *always* hungry, Xor?"

"Time flies like an arrow, and fruit flies like a banana. Let's see if there's a fruit fly problem I can help them solve."

A bell jingled as she opened the door. "Hello, hello!" the shopkeeper said. "And welcome to my shop. I'm Tinker, and you are looking for a finely crafted algorithm, am I right?"

Laurie looked at the items listed on the chalkboard, but they didn't make any sense.

```
FOR SALE              WANTED
Branch & Bound        Riemann
Convex Envelopes      ~~Poincaré~~
Karmarkar's Method    P equals NP
```

"I'm not sure. What *is* an algorithm? Can you eat it?"

"What? No, it's just a fancy way of saying 'how to do something'. But 'Algorithm' looks more impressive on the sign," said Tinker.

Xor turned orange with disappointment.

"How to do something." repeated Laurie. "In that case, I want to find a sensible way to visit every town."

"That sounds like an interesting problem. What have you been doing so far?"

Laurie told him about her adventure in the Red-Black Forest and her visit with Eponymous Bach.

"A Hamiltonian path, eh?" said Tinker. "That's a tough one. I hate to say it, because he sounds like a nice person, but the Wandering Salesman might take a long, long time to finish his tour of all the towns."

"Oh, no! But why?"

"If you always go to the nearest town you haven't visited yet, you might miss a town that's just a little farther away. Then you go to another town that's closer to you but still farther from the one you missed, and so on. You can end up criss-crossing the whole country to get to the last few towns."

"That sounds exhausting," said Laurie. The Wandering Salesman wasn't so sensible after all! "So how do I find the shortest path?"

"I'll have a look at what I have in stock. But it might be expensive."

"I don't have much money with me," Laurie said. She took a few quarters from her bag and showed them to Tinker.

He looked at them with surprise. "'Quarter Dollar.' Is this money where you come from?"

"Of course it's money! That's seventy-five cents." she said.

"Cents? We use Fair Coins here."

"What's a Fair Coin?"

"Well, they are a bit bigger than these 'Quarter Dollars' of yours, but they are not nearly as pretty! You can tell genuine Fair Coins because they always flip heads or tails, fifty-fifty."

"But you can flip quarters fifty-fifty too!"

"That may be true, but I can't just take *your* word for it, can I? Here, all Fair Coins must be certified Fair."

Laurie was crestfallen.

"Don't look so sad! I do want to help you," said Tinker. "Maybe we can do a trade. It so happens I'm in the market for a particular algorithm."

"But I don't have any algorithms, either." said Laurie.

"That's not a problem," said Tinker. "You can compose new ones any time you want, with a little bit of thinking."

"I can? How?"

"Well, everyone develops their own style. You can put little ideas together to make big ideas. Or you put two ideas side-by-side and compare them. Or you start with big ideas and take them apart."

"You mean like Eponymous does?"

"Yes, just like her. She's a great Composer."

Laurie had never thought that *she* could do things like that herself. But Tinker seemed to think it was normal.

"So what do I do?"

"The algorithm I'm looking for is how to draw a circle, Tinker said. "It's a tough one, so you'll have to use your imagination. I've asked all the adults and even Ponens and Tollens already, but all they do is mutter about X squared plus Y squared and never get anywhere."

"Take a look at this." He handed her a windup toy animal. It had a Shell, and was Round and Green. "This turtle can do three things: it can move forward or backward, it can turn, and it can draw a little dot on the paper."

"Hey, that's pretty neat!"

"Yes, but the thing is, it doesn't know how to do anything else. That's where the algorithm comes in." Tinker took out a piece of paper and wrote what looked like a little poem:

> Go forward one inch,
> make a mark,
> repeat five times.

Then he wound up the turtle and placed it on the poem. It went *zzzrbt bzzaap whuzzzsh*, and so on. Then it drew a line of dots, just like the poem said:

"You see?" Tinker said. "If you put little ideas together, you can make bigger ones," Tinker said. "And you can compose *those* ideas into even bigger and bigger ones."

"How do you do that?" asked Laurie.

"By giving them a name. You can use the name like a handle. Here, let's call the first idea LINE. Then you can put four lines together to make a square:"

LINE:
> Go forward one inch,
> make a mark,
> repeat five times.

SQUARE:
> Make a LINE.
> Make a right turn,
> repeat four times.

Make a SQUARE.

The little turtle *zzzrbt*ed and *whuzzzsh*ed and *bzzaap*ed, etc, then it drew this:

Laurie was amazed. It was like magic, but every step made sense.

"So, knowing what the turtle can do, can you teach it how to draw a circle?" Tinker said.

"I don't know," Laurie said, "but I want to try!"

"That's good enough for me. Here, you can work at my desk. There is plenty of paper and compasses and things like that."

Laurie sat down at Tinker's desk. She doodled with the compass and played with the turtle for a while, trying to remember what she knew about circles.

A circle is round. No, not just round, perfectly round. You put the pin in the center, and the pencil spins round. To make a bigger one you open the compass; to make a smaller one you close the compass. If you change the width of the compass when it's spinning, it doesn't make a circle...

Suddenly an idea, or maybe a memory, popped into her head: *A circle is all of the points that are exactly the same distance from the center.* Hmm... what if you

> Go forward one inch,
> make a mark,
> go back one inch,
> turn right a tiny bit,
> then repeat!

She wound up the little turtle again and placed it on her poem. It buzzed and burbled for a moment, then drew this:

"It's working!" she said. "Hey, it's not stopping." The turtle was drawing over dots it had already drawn.

"I think it's because you told it to repeat, but not how many times," said Tinker.

"Well, it should stop when the circle is done," Laurie said.

"It doesn't really understand circles," Tinker said. "It's just a toy turtle, remember? You have to teach it."

Laurie thought a little more, then rewrote her poem:

CIRCLE:
    Go forward one inch,
    make a mark,
    go back one inch,
    turn right *one degree*,
    repeat *three hundred sixty times*.

Then she realized that she could make circles any size she wanted. It was just like opening the compass wider:

TWO-CIRCLE:
    Go forward *two inches*,
    make a mark,
    go back *two inches*,
    turn right one degree,
    repeat three hundred sixty times.

"This is interesting. You're working really hard!" Tinker scratched his head. "But as it is, it's no good."

"Why?"

"People want to make lots of different circles," he said. "I'll have to keep a lot of algorithms of different sizes, just in case someone wants three-and-nine-thirteenths inches or four-and-three quarters."

"Well, what if you tell the turtle how big to make the circle?" she said. "Maybe like this:"

ANY-CIRCLE (*how-big?*):
> Go forward *how-big* inches,
> make a mark,
> go back *how-big* inches,
> turn right one degree,
> repeat three hundred sixty times.

"And *then*," she said, "instead of ONE-CIRCLE or TWO-CIRCLE you can say ANY-CIRCLE(one), or two, or even one-and-eleventy-sevenths!"

"Good idea, Laurie. That's a lot simpler." said Tinker. "I was worried you were going to fill my shop with circles!"

"You know, the turtle is drawing really slowly. Not like when it was doing the square," she said.

It was true. The turtle would crawl all the way to the edge of the circle, then make a mark, then crawl all the way back to the center, three hundred sixty times. With small circles it wasn't too bad, but big circles took a lot longer.

"Hmm." Tinker said. "It spends a *lot* more time running back and forth than it does making marks. Do you think you can reduce the running time?"

It makes sense, but it isn't sensible. She thought & doodled and doodled & thought, but Laurie couldn't figure out how to make it more sensible. The turtle *has* to go back to the center, right? How else could it know where the edge of the circle was?

Laurie let her eyes wander around the room. Xor was staring at a moth that was flying in lazy loops around a light bulb. His skin was slowly fading from red to yellow and back to red. The moth went round and round. It was hypnotic. Round and round and round and...

Oh.

She grabbed for a fresh piece of paper before the idea got away. *Don't let a new thing out of your sight without a name.*

MOTH-CIRCLE (*how-big?*):
　　Go forward *how-big* inches,
　　make a mark,
　　turn right one degree,
　　repeat three hundred sixty times.

Make a MOTH-CIRCLE (one).

The turtle went *bzzaap* and *zzzrbt* and *whuzzzsh* and then it started to draw. It moved one inch, made a dot, then turned a tiny bit, then moved one inch, then made another dot...

"Whoops. It's making a *huge* circle! Let me try a small number." She didn't have a small number handy, so she borrowed one she had heard from Tortoise: one thirty-second of an inch.

"That's better." Laurie said.

"Let me see," Tinker said. "Wow, look at the little guy run!"

"That was fun," said Laurie. "I didn't know you could just make up new ways to do things."

"Of course you can. Often you aren't the first to think of something, but if it works, who cares? Now, for my end of the trade."

"Did you find the shortest path?" Laurie asked.

"Not exactly. The bad news is that what you are trying to do is impossible."

"It's impossible?"

"Well, highly improbable. There are many different ways to visit all the towns. It seems like you could write an algorithm for the turtle to try each one and find the shortest, right?"

"Sure, why not?" said Laurie.

"There are twenty-one towns in Userland. How many paths do you think there are?" Tinker said.

"I don't know," said Laurie. "A hundred?"

"Way more."

"Um, a million?" Laurie said.

"More like a million million times that!" said Tinker.

"But how can that be?"

"Let's say there are only three towns: A, B, and C," Tinker said. "You are already standing in A, so you have to worry only about B and C. How many ways can you go?"

"Well," she said, "I could go from B to C, or go to C then B. That's two."

"That's right! But BC is the same as CB, just backward. Every path has a mirror image, so with three towns there is really only one possible path that visits them all. What if there were four towns, A, B, C, and D?"

Laurie counted on her fingers. "I could go BCD, or BDC, or CBD, or CDB, or DCB, or... DBC. Six! No, three."

47

"That's three times as many. Add another town, twelve times as many," Tinker said. "Add a sixth town and there are *sixty* different paths through all of them. With seven towns there are *three hundred sixty paths.* As you add more towns, the number of paths gets very big!"

3 Towns: $2 \div 2 = 1$
4 Towns: $2 \times 3 \div 2 = 3$
5 Towns: $2 \times 3 \times 4 \div 2 = 12$
6 Towns: $2 \times 3 \times 4 \times 5 \div 2 = 60$
7 Towns: $2 \times 3 \times 4 \times 5 \times 6 \div 2 = 360$
8 Towns: $2 \times 3 \times 4 \times 5 \times 6 \times 7 \div 2 = 2,520$
9 Towns: $2 \times 3 \times 4 \times 5 \times 6 \times 7 \times 8 \div 2 = 20,160$

"For twenty-one towns you have to multiply one times two times three times four, all the way up to twenty. It makes a HUGENOR-MOUS number!"

$$2 \times 3 \times 4 \times 5 \times 6 \times 7 \times 8 \times 9 \times 10 \times 11 \times 12$$
$$\times\ 13 \times 14 \times 15 \times 16 \times 17 \times 18 \times 19 \times 20 \div 2$$
$$= 1,216,451,004,088,320,000$$

"!" said Laurie.

"Indeed!" Tinker said. "All of that 'one times two times three' stuff takes too long to write. So you can use the exclamation point as a shorthand."

$$20! \div 2 = 1,216,451,004,088,320,000$$

"But that's..." Laurie said, counting the commas, "over one million million *million* paths!"

"One of those umpty-million paths is the shortest," Tinker said. "I don't know of any way to find it quickly."

"I'll be old before we check them all! Isn't there a better way?"

"Ah, that's the good news!" Tinker said. "I only deal in Exact answers. But there is a brilliant Composer who lives in Permute, named Hugh Rustic. He deals in Good Enough answers. I send him all of my hardest cases. I'll write an IOU that you can take to him."

Read Me

Laurie and Xor were halfway to Permute when a creature pulled up on a red motorcycle. On the back of the bike was a huge bag full of packages and envelopes.

"Hello, who are you?" she asked.

"I'm a daemon. Who else would I be? Hold on, there's a message for you in here somewhere." He rummaged around in his bag and handed her a plain envelope. Inside was the strangest nonsense:

> Lorem Ipsum, Esxihu! Sit amet, consectetur adipisicing elit, sed do eiusmod tempor incididunt ut labore et dolore magna aliqua. Ut enim ad minim veniam, quis nostrud exercitation...

"Are you sure this is for me?"

"Are you sure you are you?"

"Well... yes."

"Then that's for you," said the daemon. "I never make a mistake of identity."

"But how can you be sure?"

"How can you be sure you are you?"

"Because I'm right here!"

"See? It's only logical."

"But I can't read it," Laurie said. "What does it say?"

"How old are you, that you can't read?" said the daemon. "That's a real shame."

"But—"

"Did you know that kids in Finland start reading when they are only twelve months old?"

"I *can* read, I just can't read *this*. It's gibberish!"

"That," said the daemon, putting his riding gloves back on, "sounds like a whole lot of Not My Problem."

"But—"

"Do you accept delivery? Or do I have to bounce it?"

"Well, yes, but—"

"Look, Miss Well-Yes-But. I'm a mail delivery daemon. I work for the Colonel. My job is to deliver messages. What the message says is Not My Problem. Good day!" The daemon sped away, spitting dirt and gravel all over her.

"*Ooh!*" Laurie was so mad that she actually stamped her foot. "That little d-d—"

"What is it, Laurie?" asked the little lizard, who had been napping in her pocket.

"I think it's a message for me," she said. "But I don't understand it at all."

"A secret message!" Xor said, rubbing his little paws together. "It's lucky for you that my mother's half-brother is a Cryptosaurus."

"A what-asaurus?"

"A *Crypto*saurus. We know everything there is to know about secret messages. Let's see what we've got here." Xor crawled onto the message for a closer look. The paper was white, so of course his skin turned black.

"Hmm. This is a hard one. I don't recognize these letters at all."

"Why are you looking at it upside-down?"

"Of course, well, uh, sometimes you can see patterns in secret messages that way." He turned the right way round.

"Now, um, let's read it through slowly and look for clues. Con-sec-te-tour a-dee-peace-ick-ing el..." Xor's skin rippled as he moved across the letters. "...dew-is ow-tay... "

"Hey Xor, wait a second." Laurie had noticed something odd. "Back up just a little."

"Like this?"

"Yeah. Now, think really hard about blending in."

"Ok. What do you see?" he said.

"Your skin. I think I can read it."

When Xor was lined up just right, Lorem Ipsum Esxihu in black on white became **Lauren Ipsum Greetings** in white on black.

"You are un-hiding the message!"

"Really? I mean, see? I told you I could do it."

"You are wonderful, Xor! Can you get closer to the paper?"

"If I was any closer, I'd be behind it!"

Word by word they unscrambled the message. But even then it didn't make much sense:

Lauren Ipsum, Greetings! Without a doubt, you are the most interesting visitor to Userland in a long time. But you have many labors and setbacks ahead if you keep doing what you are doing. Remember, the map is not the territory!

Your Humble Servant,
Colonel Trapp

"Labors and setbacks? The map is not the territory? What does that even mean?"

"I once heard of a king who wanted to make a perfect map of his territory," said Xor.

"Why did he want to do that?"

"Kings always want something silly like a book about everything, or a chariot with no weak parts," he said. "This king decided that he wanted a perfect map as large as his kingdom. That way the royal cartographers could fit *everything* in, down to the last pebble and flower. It took seven whole years to finish it. But it was a disaster!"

"Why? What happened?" Laurie asked.

"As a map it didn't work very well. To measure the distance between two places you had to travel exactly that distance," the lizard explained. "By that time you were already there."

"Where did they even put such a big map?"

"That was the other thing. King Borges had only one kingdom so there was nowhere to put the map except right where it was. It was a huge bother, what with the map sitting on top of people's houses, and none of the crops would grow. The people finally overthrew the king and tore up the map. They say you can still see huge pieces of paper blowing around in the desert."

More Than One Way To Do It

Permute was a small village not far from Symbol. Rustic's shop was easy to find. Its sign was even bigger and fancier than Tinker's.

"Hello, Mister Rustic? Mister Tinker back in Symbol owes me an algorithm, and he said I should talk to you about it." Laurie handed him Tinker's IOU.

Rustic was a tall, loud, messy-looking man with a big red beard. He didn't look anything like the elegant Eponymous or the neat and proper Tinker. He certainly didn't look how Laurie thought a Composer should look!

"I'm, um, trying to find the shortest path through all the towns. Can you help me?"

"Wonderful! Interesting!" he said. "Tinker sent you to the right place, miss. Improbable we can do right away. Impossible, by Tuesday latest."

"But if it's impossible—" Laurie began.

"Only improbable," corrected Rustic.

"If it's *improbable*, how do you do it?"

"By shifting your point of view," said Rustic. "Instead of looking for an answer that fits your problem, you imagine an *answer* and look for a problem to fit it."

"But you can't just change the problem, can you?"

"Why, of course you can! Worrying about the problem is a waste of time! What you really want is an answer, right?"

"Maybe, but I don't understand how."

"How do you buy the best tomato?" he said.

"Well, I... what?"

"Let's say you're at the market. You want the best, most perfect tomato. But to find the *best* tomato you'd have to compare them all, right? You'd look at each and every one, turn it around, maybe squeeze it a bit. For every tomato in the whole market."

"No one does that!" said Laurie. "Well, old Mrs Harris does do that. But mom says she's a little batty. I just pick a good one."

"See? You already know how to do things the Hugh Rustic way. You don't waste your time looking for the *best* tomato when there are plenty more that are Good Enough."

"So instead of trying to find the *shortest* path through all of the towns in Userland," she said, "we look for one that's short *enough*?"

"Why not?" said Rustic. "Out of all the zippity-million paths, I bet there are a whole lot that are pretty short. You only need to find *one* of them, and that's much easier."

Rustic pulled out a large map and placed it on the counter.

"Here is where we are," he said, pointing to Permute, "and this is where you started, am I right? Let's put some pencils here to stand in for Mount Upper Bound, and a little spoon there for Lower Bound Valley." The map also had markers for Bach, Recursion Junction, and many other places she hadn't been to yet.

"Now for the fun part," said Rustic. "Let's ask the ants."

"Ask the *ants*? What are you talking about? Ants can't read maps!" Laurie said. At the mention of insects, Xor was suddenly alert.

"Who says they can't? Next you'll try to tell me that turtles can't draw circles."

"So you teach the ants to read maps?"

"Not exactly. Ants are good at finding their way home already. The idea is to get them to work for us." He opened a jar of honey and put a tiny daub of the sweet stuff on each town.

A minute passed. Nothing happened. Then a little ant crawled onto the table. It smelled the honey and zig-zagged its way onto the map. It nibbled from one bit of honey then wandered around until it walked into another one.

"When an ant finds food, she leaves a little scent message for the others that come after it," Rustic said. "Ants follow the scent of food and also the scent of other ants. Lots of ants can try lots of different paths at the same time. Eventually they'll settle on a quick route to all of the food and back to their nest."

The first ant continued on to Bach. Another appeared and went directly to Recursion instead. Still others went all the way across to Probability Bay, Permute, Notation, and other towns. Soon the map had dozens of ants going every which way, collecting bits of honey and leaving scents for their sisters.

After a few minutes it was clear that some paths were more popular than others. The lines of ants got wider and wider, until there was just one ant super-highway that marched all round the map and back to their nest. Hugh Rustic copied it to a piece of paper before the honey disappeared.

"Ah, there you go!" he said, handing Laurie his sketch.

"Thank, you Mister Rustic! Is this really the shortest way?"

"It's *a* short way. That's as much as I can promise."

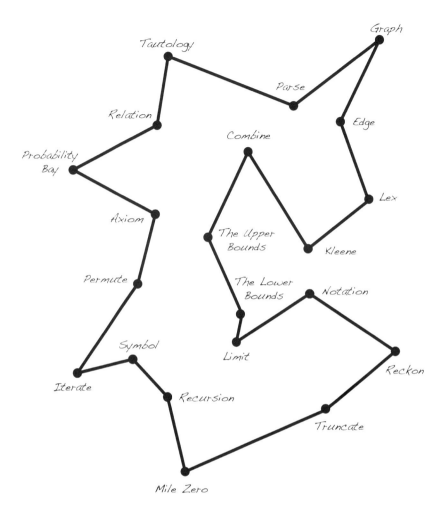

Don't Repeat Yourself

Laurie and Xor set out from Permute with their new map. They finally knew where they were, where they were going, *and* how to get there. It was all right there on paper.

"The places on this map have funny names," said Laurie. "Truncate. What's that?"

"To Truncate is to make something shorter by cutting off part of it. The town of Truncate has very precise borders." Xor said.

"Oh. So what's Axiom?" she asked.

"An Axiom is a rule that you pretend is true even if you don't know why it's true," said Xor.

"Really?"

"Surely. My cousin Nand taught me that. She's an Euclidosaurus."

"You're making stuff up again, Xor."

"No, it's just one of those things," the lizard shrugged, turning grey-green. "Either you believe in Axioms or you don't."

"Oh yeah? I bet you don't know what a Furfnoodle is." Laurie said.

"It's a... I mean, um. I give up. What is it?"

"A Furfnoodle is a kind of bird," she said. "With long blue feathers! And they love eating little lizards."

"Really?" Xor looked worried and checked the sky for blue feathers.

"No. But if I ever see a big blue bird that loves to eat lizards, I'm going to call it a Furfnoodle."

"You really shouldn't make up words like that," said Xor.

"If you can make up words, so can I," Laurie said.

"I was telling the truth, Laurie."

"It's even fun to say!" she said. "Furfnoodle."

"But—"

"Furfnooooodle!" she sang.

"Look, it's not safe—"

"Furfnoodle. Furfnoodlefurfnoodle. Furf. Nood. Ull!"

There was a *bloop* sound, and a tiny mouse-looking creature appeared on the path in front of them.

"Furfnoodle!" it said in a tiny mouse voice. It ran around them a few times then zipped off into the weeds, still screaming. *"Furfnoodle! Furfnoodle!"*

"What on earth was that?!" Laurie said.

"That," said Xor, "was a baby Jargon."

"Where did it come from? It just blooped out of the air."

"You made it with... that word."

"I *made* it?"

"I tried to warn you," Xor said. "Where did you think Jargon came from?"

"What's so special about Furf— that word?"

"It's a name that only means something to you. That's what a Jargon *is*," Xor said. "You made it. It's yours."

"But why?"

"No one knows," he said. "It's one of those Axiom things. You have to be careful with names. They have a power all their own."

A Well-Timed Entrance

Probability was a little town on the edge of the sea. It was surrounded only by a rough wooden fence, nothing like the high stone walls of Symbol. The main entrance seemed to be unguarded. Laurie was walking through the gates, when—

"Excuse me, dear! Hello, on your left." An elderly lady was sitting in the shade just inside. She held a large book on her lap. Her name tag read *Jane Hecate, Border Security*.

"Oh! I didn't see you there," said Laurie.

"That's all right, dear. But before you come in I have to make sure you are on the List."

Laurie had played this game before. "My name is Eponymous Bach, and my password is—"

"Hold on, dear, hold on! One thing at a time. First let's look up your name." She opened the heavy book and started to scan the pages with her finger, letter by letter.

"E... E... Ah, E! Here we go."

It was painfully slow.

"P... P... E-P!... E-P-O... E-P-O... no."

Jane closed the book with a thump.

"Sorry, not on the List."

"What?"

"You're not on the List, dear. There are Es, and E-Ps, but there are no names that start with E-P-O. If the *start* of your name isn't on the List, there's no reason to keep looking for the *rest* of it, now is there? It's only logical."

"But her— *my* name must be on the List! She's a great— I mean, I am—" Laurie sputtered.

"Are you a foreigner? I bet your name is spelled differently where you come from. That can happen, especially with foreigners. Why don't we try again?"

Maybe she did have an account after all. "Is it under 'Laurie Ipsum'?"

"Let me see." *Fllliiiip!* "L... L... L! A...U...R...I... Nope. Not here, but I'm sure we'll find it."

"It could be spelled Laur*en* Ipsum."

"L...A...U...R...E... No, not that way either."

"Uh, Hugh... Rustic?"

"H... H... H! H-U-G-H R-U-S-T-I-C. Ah, *there* you are."

"Great!"

"I'm so glad we could find you!" Jane said. "Your name is spelled quite a few different ways, isn't it?"

"Yeah, I guess it is. Thanks!" Laurie turned to go inside.

Jane held her back with a surprisingly strong grip.

"Your *password*, dear?"

"Oh! Is it 'Rustic'?"

"No."

"Turtle?"

"No."

"Algorithm?"

"A...L... No."

"Good Enough?"

"No."

Laurie was stumped. *"Now what?"* she whispered to Xor. *"She doesn't care if I try every word in the dictionary. But we'll be here all month!"*

"*I have an idea,*" Xor whispered back. "*Try Abstraction.*"

"*What is that? I don't even—*"

"*My third cousin is a Thesaurus. Trust me!*"

"Is it Ab-stract-tion?" Laurie said.

"A...B...S... No, dear."

"*Trust me, huh?*" she said.

"*Come to think of it, I never liked that cousin.*"

"*Hey... did you notice something?*"

"*Is it dinner time already?*"

"*No! When I said Turtle she said no right away,*" Laurie said.

"*So? It's not the password,*" Xor said.

"*But when I said Algorithm, she took longer to say no. And with Abstraction she took a little longer than that, moving her finger over the page...*" Laurie cleared her throat and spoke to Jane. "Is the password, um, About?"

"A...B...O... No."

"*See?*" she whispered.

"*OK, but what does it mean?*"

"*Maybe that means the real password starts with AB! So if we keep guessing AB words...*"

Letter by letter they cracked Rustic's password. Laurie did not know many of the words Xor suggested but he swore they were real, on the honor of Thesauruses everywhere. She knew she was getting warmer because Jane would take longer and longer to say no to her guesses.

"Abend!"

"A...B...E... No."

"Abdicate!"

"A...B...D... No."

"Abrograte!"

"A...B...R...O... No."

"*It starts with ABR!*" Laurie whispered.

"Abrupt!"

"A...B...R...U... No."

"Abraid!"

"A...B...R...A...I... No."

"*We're getting close,*" Xor said in her ear. "*What starts with ABRA?*"

"Abracadabra?" Laurie said out loud.

"A-B-R-A-C-A-D-A-B-R-A!" said Jane. "That's the password, right as rain. Welcome to Probability!"

A Fair Exchange

The first thing Laurie tried to do in Probability was buy a sweetbread, but her strange money wasn't any good. Nobody wanted her "Quarter Dollars". Nobody wanted any algorithms either.

"Message for you." A red daemon carrying a mail bag appeared out of nowhere on the street.

"For me?" she said.

"You don't see me talking to anyone else, do you?"

Xor made short work of the gibberish in the message. This one was shorter and more useful.

> Laurie, you continue to surprise me. I wonder if a bank can help with your money problems.
>
> Col. Trapp

Laurie rushed back to a building she remembered walking past: The Fair Coin Savings & Loan. She stepped inside. It looked just like banks back home.

"Why are we at a bank?" asked Xor.

"Because I'm getting hungry. It's almost dinner time."

"Finally. But you can't eat money!"

"I can't spend it either."

Laurie walked up to the teller window and put everything money-like she had on the counter: a few dollar bills, three quarters, a penny, a dime, and her lucky poker chip.

"Excuse me, sir?"

"Yes?" The teller was a tall thin man with round glasses. A little card said his name was Trent Escrow.

"I'm from a foreign country and I want to know what these are worth."

"Hmm! I've never seen these coins before! And what are these fancy little pieces of paper supposed to be?"

"That's money, too. One dollar." Laurie said.

"Money made of *paper*," Trent said. "How strange! They are very pretty, but I'm sorry to say they are worthless here."

"Oh no, really? Why?"

"You can't flip a piece of *paper* fifty-fifty, now can you? But these coins are remarkable," he said, examining the poker chip carefully and flipping it a few times.

"Are *they* worth anything?"

"Well, they look pretty balanced to me. But they aren't certified Fair, so no one will take them at face value."

"Tinker said the same thing, but I don't understand," said Laurie. "Where I come from, you can flip quarters fifty-fifty, no problem."

"Ah, but one side might be a *little* different from the other," Trent said, "so it might not be exactly even."

"Really?"

"Surely. The unfairness shows up better if you spin the coin instead of flipping it. That's how we test all of our Fair Coins."

"So my coins are worthless too?"

"Not quite. I can give you an exchange rate: two of your coins for one Fair Coin."

"Why two to one?" she asked.

"Good question!" Trent said. "Most people don't know this, but it's possible to get absolutely Fair flips out of even the most unfair coin."

"I don't believe you."

"Here, let me show you." Trent reached into his drawer and handed her a large, heavy coin. "This is a fake Fair Coin. It looks just like a real one, doesn't it? But it's easy to tell it's fake because it comes up Heads a lot more than Tails."

"So how do you get a fair flip?"

"Just flip it twice. If you get Heads-Tails, use Heads as your answer. If it comes up Tails-Heads, use Tails as your answer. If you get Heads-Heads or Tails-Tails, just start over."

"Oh, I see. The unfairness cancels itself out!"

"Right you are. No matter how unfair a coin is, the odds of getting Heads then Tails will always be *exactly* the same as getting Tails then Heads."

Trent Escrow solemnly exchanged her five coins and lucky poker chip for three Fair Coins.

"And that's why the rate is two to one."

"Thank you!" Laurie rushed outside to catch the baker before he closed. Dinner!

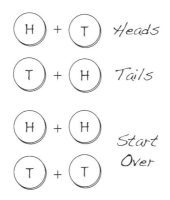

An Improbable Twist

"Got you!" A fat policeman grabbed Laurie by the collar. "Why are you running? Did you rob the bank too?"

"What? Who are you? Let me go!"

"I'm Officer Custody, and *you* are in big trouble," the policeman said. "Lauren Ipsum, IF that is your real name, I arrest you on charges!"

"What charges? What are you talking about?"

"That doesn't matter!" he shouted in her ear, shaking her around. "Charges!"

"Ow! But what charges?" His hold on her was painful. People on the street were starting to point and stare. If there ever was a time Laurie wished she could disappear like a Steganosaurus, it was now!

"You're going to be difficult? Let's do it nice and proper, if you insist!" Custody took out a roll of paper and cleared his throat.

"Lauren Ipsum, you are under arrest for Attempted Mythology, Counterfeiting Fair Coins, *two* counts of Impersonating a Composer, Hacking in the Third Degree, and Miscellaneous Mopery With Intent to Creep!"

"Let me go! You're the creep!" Laurie tried to twist away, but his grip was too strong.

"Hey, Custody! Why are you beating up on little girls?"

A tough-looking woman stepped out of the crowd to confront the policeman. She wore big boots, black gloves, and an eyepatch in the shape of a heart.

"This isn't a girl, Losesome. This is a dangerous criminal! She broke through our perimeter security," the policeman said.

"You mean Jane, that little old lady at the gate?"

"Officer Hecate, yes!"

"Come on, Custody. Jane isn't hard to fool. Last week I told her I was Santa Claus." People in the crowd chuckled.

"That's beside—"

"And what the heck is 'Attempted Mythology'? I think you just made that up."

"What? I—"

"How do you even know you have the right person?"

"She matches the description!"

"Really? She doesn't look like Santa Claus to me!"

"NO," he said. "She matches the description of the hacker who came through this afternoon!"

"So you are saying a child was able to get through all of your super-duper security?" she said.

"Well—"

"Anyway, this girl is my assistant."

By now Custody was thoroughly confused. "This little... she works for *you?*"

"Of course. She's helping me test the security of this place. And if a *child* can run circles around you..." She shook her head. "Let's say it doesn't look good."

"But you're—"

The woman said nothing. She only smiled, showing a lot of teeth.

Custody was suddenly sweating. He let go of Laurie and pulled out a handkerchief.

"Hey, now, it was an honest mistake! I didn't know she worked for the Col— um, you."

"Well now you do. And now we're leaving. Come on, Laurel." The woman took her by the arm and walked away, head high.

"*Let's just walk away slowly,*" the woman whispered. "*When we turn the corner, try to make it to the marina before Custody starts using his brain instead of his mouth.*"

As soon as they were out of sight they broke into a run.

"That was great! But my name is Laurie, not Laurel."

"Close enough. I'm Winsome Losesome."

"It's nice to meet you! Thank you for helping me! I didn't mean to cause trouble."

"Don't mention it. I was leaving town anyway. And I really don't like that guy. He's a dumb bully."

At the marina, Winsome jumped aboard a boat and went to work getting it ready to depart.

"Come on! Hop on," she said.

"Whose boat is this, Winsome?"

"It's my boat, the *Doppelganger*. Get that other rope, would you?"

"Wow, how did you get a boat? Are you a pirate?"

"I'm a lot of things, girl." Winsome said. "As for the boat, I kind of stole it. But I stole it honestly!"

"How can you steal something *honestly*?" Laurie was afraid that she was getting into even more trouble.

"I used to be a deckhand on this boat," she said. "The Boss made me do all of the dirty work. *Losesome, replace the main mast!* He'd say. *Put a new rigger on the widdershins!*"

Winsome unfurled the sail.

"But secretly, I was saving all the old parts I replaced. They were going to the trash anyway, so might as well keep them, right? Once I collected enough pieces, I quit, and put them back together into a boat. Boss never found out, either! The boat he has is all replacement parts. A copy. I have the *real* one."

"But—"

"Think about it later, sweetie? We're busy running from the Law."

She had a point. Laurie untied the rope and they cast off into the moonless night.

The Game of Life

The *Doppelganger* sailed out of Probability Bay and far away from their troubles. Laurie risked a peek over the side of the boat and caught a beautiful surprise.

"Winsome! Look at that!"

In the wake of the boat, glowing sparkles lit up the water. Blue and green curlicues danced behind them as the waves fanned out.

"Oh, yeah. Those are called gliders. Pretty, aren't they?"

"They're beautiful! What makes them glow?"

"When you stir up the water, it makes them glow and form patterns. You can see them on only a dark night like this."

"Wow! I've never seen anything like this!"

"Want to see something really cool?" Winsome dipped a shallow pan into the water and set it on a bench. After it settled down, she traced a little figure in the water.

The glowing dots came alive and wiggled around the pan a few times before fading away.

"How do they move like that? Are they really alive?"

"I don't think so. It's just a pattern that looks alive. There are supposed to be some rules about how the glow moves around, but I never paid attention. Maybe you can figure it out."

Winsome went back to minding the wheel. Laurie played with making more gliders, pretty waves, and curls. She got good at finding patterns that skittered through the water for longer and longer.

Xor tried to bite the glowing squiggles as they wriggled by, but all he caught was a mouthful of water.

"Winsome, where are we going?"

"We're headed for Abstract Island," she said. "I have some deliveries to make. We should get there by morning."

"Abstract Island? That isn't on my map," Laurie said.

"I bet a lot of things aren't on your map, girl."

"You mean the map is not the territory?"

"Eh? Who told you that?"

"Colonel Trapp. He sent me a really strange letter."

"Oh, *him*."

"Do you know Colonel Trapp?"

"He's a crazy old man," Winsome said. "Always messing around in other people's business. Sending those rude daemons with his stupid secret messages."

"The secret messages were fun. Xor figured out how to—"

"Be careful with the Colonel, Laurie. I'm pretty sure he was the one trying to get you thrown in jail."

"Who is he?" Laurie asked.

"He's my— he was my boss," said Winsome. "This was his mail boat. Until I copied it. We... disagree about how to do business, so I struck out on my own."

"You had a fight with him?"

"Well, yes." Winsome said.

"What did you fight about?"

"He wants things to stay just the way they are. I... don't."

"Oh," said Laurie. Something about Winsome's voice told Laurie not to ask her more about the fight. They were quiet for a time, watching the sky and water.

"He's right about one thing," Winsome said softly. "The Colonel."

"What's that?"

"A map is just a picture. It's not the real thing. If someone forgets to put Abstract Island on a map, the Island still exists. It doesn't care what you know."

"No one in Userland said anything about islands," Laurie said.

"The people back there don't know much about the world outside. That's the way the Colonel likes it. Userland is an island. It's a whole world of islands."

Laurie didn't like what she was hearing. "But Winsome, I have to follow my map to get back home."

"Do you?"

"Yes!"

"Why?"

"That's what everyone told me to do," Laurie said.

"That's not a good enough reason," Winsome said.

"It isn't?" People told Laurie what to do all the time. She didn't always do it, of course. But there was always the feeling that she was wrong for not doing something she was told to.

"No! You should always know *why* you are doing something," said Winsome, "and not just because someone told you to do it. Keep your head on and be flexible, girl. Otherwise you are like those little gliders, going wherever people send you."

"But Tinker said—"

"Forget Tinker for a minute," Winsome said. "How did you get lost in the first place?"

"I had a fight with my mom," Laurie said. "Mom wants me to go to school over the summer, but I don't even need to!" Laurie said.

"Maybe summer school is a good thing. I heard that kids in Finland—"

"I don't care! I don't want to waste the whole summer in school with people I don't even know!"

"Ok, that's fair. So then what happened?"

"I took a walk in the woods to calm down a little, but I was so mad that I forgot to watch where I was going, and I got lost, and I spent a long time walking in circles," Laurie said, tears leaking. "Then I was attacked by those Jargon things, and I ran and ran until I came here, but then I made a Jargon myself because I didn't know the rules, and no one here has even heard of Hamilton, or dollars, or anything! And I don't understand why I need a password, and now I'm going to an island that's not even on the map and—"

"Hey, slow down—" Winsome said.

"—now I'm lost all over again and... and..." Laurie started sobbing.

"Wait, don't, oh man..."

Winsome knew how to handle the nastiest people you'd never want to meet, but a crying girl was something else. She gave Laurie an awkward hug until the noise stopped.

"You done?"

"Yeah." *Sniff!*

"Good. I thought you were going to sink the boat," said Winsome. "Why don't you go below and get some rest? And think about something before you fall sleep."

"Think about what?"

"Making your own map."

In the Abstract

"Laurie, wake up."

"Mrfl."

"Come on. Wake up."

"Mom?" It felt way too early to wake up. Laurie heard water splashing. The bath?

"We're here, girl. Help me tidy up the boat."

"The... boat? What b—" she opened her eyes. The walls were made of wood. She was on the *Doppelganger*.

Laurie went above and got her first look at the island. The little harbor was a perfect half-moon. They were tied up at the end of the main pier. All around, people were fishing or fussing around on their identical-looking boats. Houses and shops were scattered among trees and hilly parks.

"Hey, all of the buildings look the same. And the trees, too!"

"That's how they do things here. First they talk *endlessly* about what makes a building, or a street, or a pigeon. Once they find the perfect abstract design, they make a bunch of copies. Let's go get some breakfast and deliver these letters."

Winsome lifted a huge mail bag and headed down the pier. Laurie had to hurry to keep up.

Many restaurants were nearby the harbor. There was the Philosopher's Diner, packed with old people wearing togas. At Random Slice Pizza you never knew what toppings you'd get. It was too early for pizza, though. They took a booth at the Push & Pop Café and ordered full stacks of pancakes.

"Why are you eating your pancakes funny?"

"I'm not eating them funny." Instead of cutting through the whole pile of pancakes, Winsome ate them off the top of the stack, one by one. "You're eating them funny."

"What should I do about my map?" Laurie said between bites.

"Beats me, girl." Winsome said. "So let's play a game."

"What game?"

"It's called Five Whys. It's a game to play when you get stuck."

"How do you play?"

"I ask you a Why question, and you answer, then I ask you another, until we find the reason you got stuck," Winsome said.

"For example?"

"For example, why do you want to follow that map?"

"It's the one Hugh Rustic made for me with his ants," Laurie said. "He found a short-enough path through all of the towns."

"So why did you want to find a short-enough path?"

"Because there are blippity-million paths through Userland, and Tinker didn't know how to find the *shortest* one." Laurie said.

"Why did you ask Tinker for the shortest path?"

"Because Eponymous said that the Wandering Salesman's algorithm —well, she didn't say algorithm, I figured that out later— she said his algorithm wasn't sensible."

"Why did you want to use the Salesman's algorithm?"

"Because that's how he finds his way home."

"Why did you think his algorithm made sense for you?"

"Because, I..." Laurie hadn't thought about it. "...I don't know."

"You were lost and scared, and he seemed to know what he was doing, right?"

"Yeah, I guess so."

"Sweetie, the Wandering Salesman is a *salesman*. He has to visit many places to buy and sell," Winsome said. "And it's his job to convince people."

"Eponymous said that it made sense, though."

"His algorithm makes sense for him, but maybe not for you. It's tempting to jump on the first answer that comes along. But a lot of the time it's not the best. That's why you have to keep your head on."

"Why didn't anybody say anything?"

"Because it's up to you to ask the right questions," said Winsome. "No one is going to live your life for you, girl."

"But I asked everyone how to get home!"

"No, it sounds like you drifted away from your real goal. By the time you got to Rustic, you didn't ask how to find Hamilton. You asked him how to find a short path through all the towns in Userland."

"Wow, you're right." Laurie looked down at her lap. "I feel really stupid now."

"Nah, don't feel bad. Everyone makes that mistake."

"They do?"

"You have no idea," said Winsome. "Algorithms don't just happen in turtles and ants and coins. They also happen inside your head, and those are the hardest to get right."

"I still don't know how I'm going to get home."

"Neither do I. But asking the right question is a good start. And as long as you're here, you might as well be useful." Winsome pointed out the window to a tall white tower on a hill. "Do you see that lighthouse?"

"What about it?"

"Would you like to go up to the top? The view is amazing."

"Well... sure! That sounds like fun."

"Great. Take this." Winsome handed her a heavy wooden box. "I need you to deliver it to the lighthouse keeper."

"What is it?"

"It's very expensive. And fragile."

"But—"

"Go on, he's waiting. I'll meet you back at the boat."

———

The climb up the hill was exhausting. There wasn't a doorbell or anyone on the ground floor, so Laurie shouted at the tower.

"Hello! Hello up there! Anyone?"

A voice came floating down. "Yes! Come up! The door is open."

Round and round and up the staircase, Laurie huffed and puffed with the unwieldy box. Finally she came to the watchman's room at the top of the tower, completely out of breath. The room had no walls to speak of; it was made almost entirely of glass.

The lighthouse keeper had his back to her, scanning the horizon with binoculars.

"Oh, good. Put it down carefully."

Laurie heaved the box onto a bench, then stood next to the lighthouse keeper to get a better look out the windows. To one side was the wide blue water. She could barely see a bump on the horizon. Maybe that was Userland. To the other side, all of Abstract Island was laid out like, well, like a map. There was the port and the *Doppelganger*. Two people in togas were arguing in front of the Philosopher's Diner. From above, the island looked even more neat and organized.

"Wow! You can see everything from here!"

"Yes."

"So... that's it?"

"That's it," said the keeper. "Oh, er, thank you."

Walking downhill, without the box, was a lot easier than going up.

"What *was* in that box, anyway?" she wondered out loud.

"My guess is lightbulbs. Something boring," said Xor. "Adults are always making a fuss over boring things."

———

Back at the boat, Winsome was getting ready to sail again.

"Good work, girl. Thanks."

"You're welcome. He didn't talk much."

"That's how some people get, living in a tower all the time," Winsome said. "Other people start to talk a *lot*."

"They do?"

"You'll see. So what are you going to do now?"

"I thought about it," Laurie said. "Userland is just one island. This island is... nice, but I asked around, and no one here has heard of Hamilton either."

"Well," said Winsome, "do you want to be my assistant?"

"What do you mean?"

"You're looking for a way home, right? The *Doppelganger* goes just about everywhere. You can help me make deliveries, and you'll be able to look for answers in a lot more places than you could by walking. Or swimming."

"Isn't that the same as you telling me where to go?"

Winsome smiled. "You're getting smarter by the minute. But don't get too smart. Sail with me for a while. I need the help. If you don't like it, I'll drop you off wherever you want. No hard feelings."

Cleverness When It Counts

Travelling with Winsome on the *Doppelganger* was lots of fun. Laurie got to see so many strange places and people that sometimes she forgot she was trying to find her way back to Hamilton. But her job wasn't easy.

When they arrived at an island, Winsome would take a huge bag of letters into town and deliver them. She would return a few hours later with a new load of letters to take from that island to somewhere else.

Laurie's job was to deliver the interesting packages. (She kept using that word. Laurie didn't think it meant what Winsome thought it meant.) "Interesting" customers lived in tall towers in the middle of nowhere, over shaky scary bridges, on top of high hills, or on the sides of cliffs. The packages were heavy. (And fragile. And expensive.) The directions were often bizarre and incomplete. Just to make it there and back in one piece, Laurie had to be clever about her work.

This time the package Laurie was supposed to deliver didn't have a proper address at all. It said *FIRST, FOLLOW THE BYZANTINE PROCESS*. Winsome had gone off somewhere else, so she couldn't ask for help.

"What is The Byzantine Process? I don't even know what it looks like. How can I follow it?" she said.

"We're on the Island of Byzantium," said Xor, "so the Process must be the name of the main road. Or a river. Or a road beside the river. It's only logical."

"You have no idea, do you, Xor?"

"Sure I do! My stepsister is an Atlasaurus!"

"What's an Atlas... never mind. I don't want to know."

Where to begin was no mystery, at least. The entrance to Byzantium was blocked by an enormous stone building. *All Deliveries Enter*

Here, a sign said. A long red carpet led inside to a semantic turnstile with two guards, just like in Symbol. The guards seemed to be in the middle of an argument.

"...that makes no sense, Anton!"

"It makes perfect sense, Basil. If you only—"

"Excuse me," said Laurie. "I'd like to pass through."

"Sorry, miss. For that you must have a Pass signed by the Junior Officer of the Watch—" began Anton.

"—and countersigned by the Senior Officer of the Watch." Basil finished.

"Who are they?" she asked.

"We are."

"Oh, good."

"Lieutenant Basil is the Junior Officer of the Watch, and I am the Senior Officer of the Watch—" said Anton.

"—only on even-numbered days," said Basil. "On odd-numbered days I'm the Senior Officer and Lieutenant Anton is the Junior."

"What day is it today?"

"That's what we were discussing before you interrupted," Anton said. "Yesterday was the Thirtieth of Pentember. I think we all agree that thirty is an even number, and so I was the Senior Officer."

"That means today is the Zeroth of Hectember," said Basil.

The Zeroth of...? Well, everything has to start somewhere, Laurie thought. "So Anton should be Junior today, and Basil should be Senior, right?"

"It's not as simple as that, miss!" said Anton.

"There is the question of whether zero is even or odd," said Basil.

"Oh." Laurie had never thought of zero that way. Now she was curious. "So which is it? Even or odd?"

"Zero is even!" said Anton. "It evenly divides by two. Zero divided by two is zero."

"That doesn't prove a thing," said Basil. "Zero divided by *any* number is zero. More to the point, if zero is even then Anton would have two days in a row as Senior Officer, and I won't stand for that!"

"Even more to the point," said Anton, "if zero is odd then Basil would be Senior both today and tomorrow, the First of Hectember. I won't sit still for *that*!"

"You see miss, when it comes to important questions, where you stand depends on where you sit." Basil said.

"But—"

"Anyway, you need to have your Pass Approval Request Form approved first."

"My Pass Approval Request Form? I don't understand."

"Oh, we don't have the Passes here, of course," said Basil. "That would be bad security!"

"You have to get your Pass Approval Request approved by General Case. If he says you can pass, then we say you can pass." said Anton.

"He's down the hall to the right," added Basil. "Now see here, Anton: any odd number multiplied by itself is even, and every even number multiplied by itself is also even. So multiplication doesn't prove it either..."

Laurie walked down an endless hall until she came to one marked *General Constantin Case, Office of Perimeter Security.*

"Hello, Mister General, sir? I'm looking for a Pass to pass through the gate."

"Hmm. And what is your business?"

"I'm delivering a package."

"Hmm. How many fenceposts do I need for a hundred feet of fence?"

"Excuse me?"

"*Fenceposts*, child. I want to put a fencepost every ten feet for a hundred feet of fence. How many do I need?"

"Uh, ten?"

"That's what I thought too," he said, "but we're running short. I suspect the enemy is stealing them."

Laurie had no idea what he was talking about. "I'm sorry to bother you sir, but about that Pass..."

"Take this to General Darius down the hall," said Case, handing her a blank Pass Approval Request Form. "If he approves it, I'll approve it."

"Thank you!" she said brightly.

"Hmm."

———

General Damien Darius (Office of Logistics) was also busy with a stack of paperwork. A large map of a river was covered in scribbles and arrows.

"General Darius? I need a Pass." said Laurie, handing him the Pass Approval Request Form she got from Case.

"Are you here about the mandelbroccoli?"

"Uh, mandelbroccoli? No sir."

"Then you have information regarding the wolf."

"The wolf?"

"Yes, the wolf," said Darius. "One of my men is trying to move a wolf, a goat, and a load of mandelbroccoli across the Concurrent Streams. The boat is only big enough for him and one other thing."

"Can't he take one at a time?" she asked.

94

"No good. If he takes the wolf and leaves the goat alone with the broccoli, she'll eat it. If he takes the broccoli and leaves the wolf with the goat, the wolf will eat *her*."

"So take the goat first," said Laurie, doing a pantomime in her head. "And then take... oh."

"Yes. No matter what he takes next, he has the same problem on the other side." Darius said.

"That's terrible news, but I'm actually asking about a Pass."

"And I don't have time for civilian chit-chat. Take whatever this is to General Euripides in the Office of Records," he said, handing back her Form. "If he approves it, I'll approve it."

Down the hall she went.

———

Euripides had his hands full with a problem of his own. People were crowded around huge record books lying on tables in the Office of Records. Some people were trying to read long strings of numbers from the books. Others wanted to *write* new numbers in the books. The readers and writers were thrashing about, getting in each other's way. It looked like a fight could start at any time.

The General was pacing from table to table, listening to complaints and issuing orders. A crowd of people followed him around, shouting over each other, trying to get his attention. It looked like he barely had time to think.

Laurie pushed and struggled and wiggled her way to the front of the crowd.

"Sir? General Euripides? Can you help me?"

"Eh? Oh, another one. Are you a reader or a writer?"

"I'm not a reader or a writer. I need you to app—" but the General had to go break up an argument.

"Now what was it you wanted? A reader? Which book?"

"No sir. I need— sir? Hello, sir?" Euripides was off to another corner of the room. She tried to get the General's attention again, but the crowd kept shoving her out of the way.

———

Laurie sat on the floor in the hallway and put her head on her knees, exhausted and confused. Broccoli, fenceposts, Passes, General This, General That... where did it all end? She could still hear the fighting over who got to use what book next.

"Those people are so rude. Why can't they take turns and share?"

"Maybe nobody taught them how," Xor said. "My cousin Rex never liked to share. Of course, he was forty feet tall and had teeth as long as your arm."

"Somebody should teach them. It's not fair."

"Yeah." Xor said. "Hey, aren't you Somebody?"

"Me?"

"Yeah! I'm pretty sure you are Somebody. Otherwise you'd be Nobody, and that wouldn't make sense to Anybody."

"But I'm just a kid. No one pays attention to kids."

"So? No one pays attention to me either," he said.

"But that's what you want, right? To be invisible."

"Oh. Yeah."

"What are we going to do, Xor?"

"I dunno. Think. You're good at that."

"No, I'm not."

"Really? Tinker thought you are. Winsome does, too."

Laurie put her head down again and sighed. "I'm just her delivery girl."

"No, you're her *interesting* delivery girl," Xor said.

"So?"

"So you figure out how to go where other people can't. Remember when you were arguing with Ponens and Tollens outside of Symbol? I didn't think you'd find a way past them. But you did. Same with that scary old lady Jane."

"They never caught us either," Laurie smiled a little.

"Not until Custody grabbed you."

"And that's when Winsome saved— oh."

"What?"

"I can't go back and tell Winsome that I couldn't even get past the front door!"

"Why not?"

"I just... I can't. She gave me a job and I have to do it myself."

So with nothing else she could do, and nowhere else to go, Laurie started to think.

She needed an Approval from Euripides so she could get one from Darius, use *that* to get one from General Case, to be signed and countersigned by Basil and Anton. There was something familiar about this Byzantine chaos. Something Hugh Rustic had told her. *Think of an answer, and then look for a problem that fits.*

Euripides was up to his ears with problems. Everyone wanted to do everything at once. Maybe she should start there...

———

A half hour later Laurie was back in the Office of Records. She didn't shout, or shove, or cut in front of anyone. She waited. Eventually one of the books became completely free. Laurie walked over to it and drew a line on the floor.

A woman came over to write in the book. Laurie stepped aside and let her work. A few moments later a man came up to read from the book.

"New policy, sir," said Laurie. "You have to stand on the line until the first customer is finished."

"But I have to look up something on page 1728!"

"I'm sorry," she said. "General's Orders. But you're next."

"Oh. All right then." The man stood carefully on the line. Another person came to read from page 1024.

"General's Orders," said 1728, pointing to the line. "Don't worry. You're right after me."

Laurie held the line until the pattern looked like it would keep going on its own. Each new person would be told to wait by the others already in line. Then she waited for the next book to open up.

As the idea spread, people started drawing lines of their own in front of other books. Soon the whole Records Office was calm and organized. After all, it was General's Orders.

Euripides almost couldn't believe what he was seeing. The readers and writers were following a simple rule and taking turns! He was glad to have a rest, and signed Laurie's Pass without a second thought.

———

"General Darius?"

"You again. I don't want to hear about anything else until we've sorted out the Broccoli Situation."

"I think the mandelbroccoli doesn't matter, sir." said Laurie.

"What? You want the goat to eat it all?"

"No, I mean the answer is the same even if you had two wolves instead. You can't leave the goat alone with anything. If you change your point of view, it's easy. I think."

"Go on," said the General.

Laurie thought a little more, then wrote down her idea. It looked a bit like the algorithms back at Tinker's:

1. Take the goat over to the other side.
2. Come back empty.
3. Take the wolf over, but *bring back the goat.*
4. Leave the goat and take the mandelbroccoli over.
5. Come back empty.
6. And finally, take the goat over again!

Darius studied her poem for a while, his hands moving this way and that as he thought it through.

"I believe this will work. The goat won't like going back and forth so much, but it's better than getting eaten," said Darius. "Now what is it you wanted, miss?"

———

"General Case, sir? General Darius signed my Pass."

"Hmm," he hmmed, scribbling a signature below Darius's.

"Thank you, sir."

"Hmm."

"Sir? One more thing."

"Hmm?"

"I don't think anyone is stealing your fenceposts. It's just that you need *eleven* posts. Like this:"

1 2 3 4 5 6 7 8 9 10 11

| 1 | 2 | 3 | 4 | 5 | 6 | 7 | 8 | 9 | 10 |

"Hmm!"

———

"Welcome back, miss," said Anton. Laurie handed over the paperwork she'd collected from the Byzantine Generals.

"It looks like everything is in order," said Basil, examining the list of signatures. "These approvals go all the way to the top!"

"Have you anything to declare, miss?" asked Anton.

"Declare?"

"What Lieutenant Anton means," said Basil, "is there anything we should know about."

"Oh. Well, I think Anton is right. Zero is even."

"No!" said Basil.

"Yes. Zero can't be odd because one is odd, and you can't have two odd numbers in a row, right?"

"Right!" said Anton.

"I suppose not," Basil grumped. "But that doesn't prove it's even."

"Well, if you add an odd number and an even number together, you always get an odd number." said Laurie.

"Um," Basil ummed, thinking about it. "One plus two is three, two plus three is five... yes."

"So I can prove whether zero is even or odd. Add it to an odd number and see what you get," she said. "Zero plus one is one, and one is odd. So zero must be even," said Laurie.

"I'm still not convinced," said Basil.

"OK," she said. "If you add two *even* numbers together, you always get an even number, right? Zero plus two is two, which is even. Zero is even again!"

"Exactly!" Anton said.

"Hrmph," Basil hrmphed. "So zero is even. How do I keep Anton from being Senior two days in a row?"

"That's the easy part," Laurie said. "The problem is that yesterday the Thirtieth and today the Zeroth are both even. Anton was the Senior yesterday. So Basil, you can be the Senior Officer of the Watch today."

"Now hang on a minute—" said Anton.

"—but only until lunchtime," said Laurie. "After lunch today, Anton is Senior. That way it's fair."

"Brilliant!" said Senior Officer Basil. "Junior Officer Anton, sign this young lady's Pass!"

Approved, approved, approved, signed, and countersigned. Laurie was finally through the turnstile.

"I'm glad that's over," said Xor. "Now, where the heck is that Byzantine Process?"

A Change of Plan

SECOND, it said, *DELIVER TO BRUTO FUERZA, LOOKOUT HILL LIGHTHOUSE*. Laurie and Xor couldn't see any lighthouse, but there was a cloud of dust rising from the hill.

"You work for Winsome, eh? Right on time." said Bruto when they arrived. "I'm sorry to say we're behind schedule. Our lighthouse isn't finished. We've been working double-time, day and night."

"Are you going to put the lighthouse on top of that castle?"

"Castle?" said Bruto. "That *is* the lighthouse."

Dozens of Green Shelled Round machines were busy all round the enormous structure. They looked just like Tinker's turtle, but they were the size of a large truck. Instead of drawing dots on paper these turtles were laying bricks on top of bricks, making WALLs, STAIRs, and WINDOWs right before her eyes.

"What are all those things coming out from the wall?" she asked, pointing to a forest of supports and buttresses on one side of the tower.

"We've had no end of problems," said Bruto, shaking his head and spitting. "The south wall was falling outward. So we had to shore it up. Then it started falling *inward*."

"Is that why you are behind schedule?" she asked. There was something about the scene that bothered Laurie, but she couldn't put her finger on it. It looked... messy.

"Things are always going wrong," Bruto said. "Big ideas come with big risks. But we can fix any problem with more power and hard work!"

"You certainly have a lot of both," Laurie said, with just a teensy tiny bit of envy. The things she could do with all those turtles! "How do you teach the turtles to build a tower?"

102

"Here, let me show you." Bruto led her to a tent nearby. A small army of people was working around a table. "First we write the plans on paper:"

BRICK-LINE:
  Lay a brick,
  move forward,
  lay a brick,
  move forward,
  lay a brick,
  move forward,
    ...

"That part makes a LINE of bricks. We stack a bunch of BRICK-LINES on top of each other, and that's how a wall gets built. To make the wall thicker, we just add more commands."

BRICK-LINE-VERSION-TWO:
  Lay a brick,
  lay a brick,
  move forward,
  lay a brick,
  lay a brick,
  move forward,
  lay a brick,
  lay a brick,
  move forward,
  lay a brick,
  lay a brick,
    ...

"Wow, it just goes on and on and on," said Laurie, flipping through the pages. "It must have taken forever to write all of this."

"Big buildings need big plans. Big plans need big teams. It's only logical," Bruto said. "Writing the plans wasn't the worst part, though. We're running out of bricks!"

"Really? But why?"

"The first version wasn't strong enough, and it fell down. So now I'm making a tower twice as big, twice as thick, and twice as tall. Two times two times two is eight."

"So it needs eight times as many bricks?" she asked.

"It's just a matter of supplies."

"How do you know this version of the plan will work?"

"We're not a bunch of amateurs, girlie. We do extensive testing of our algorithms." Bruto said. "Take a look at this!" Off to the side was a table covered with tiny turtles and tiny bricks.

"Hey, they are building a tower too!" Sure enough, the turtles were following the same plan as their bigger cousins.

"We test new plans by building a scale model."

"But Bruto, the model doesn't have the same extra stuff keeping the walls from falling down."

"Some problems only show up in the full size. When that happens we have to adapt."

"Oh," Laurie said. "But if the model is not the same as the real thing, how can you be sure that—"

CRACK!

They turned around just in time to see the full-size tower collapse into a big pile of bricks. Bruto stood still for a long time, watching the dust settle as the turtles got to work cleaning up the mess.

"Are you going to make it even bigger now?" Laurie asked.

"No. What we need... what we need is a radical change of plan! All right, everyone," Bruto said to no one in particular, "Clear the decks! Empty your minds! Brainstorm! I want new ideas!"

"*Let's make the walls four times as thick, but the tower only three times as high.*" said one.

"*More supports inside and out!*" said another.

"*Use bigger bricks!*"

"*Make bricks out of steel!*"

"*Steel is too expensive. How about iron?*"

"*Are you crazy? Iron will rust!*"

"*I told you we should have used a triangle.*"

"*Make the outside out of steel, but the inside out of bricks.*"

"Good! This is good! Keep them coming. We're thinking out of the box. Anyone else?"

"Why not a circle, like the lighthouse on Abstract Island?" Laurie said. She thought about it for a minute, then wrote out a pair of little poems.

> BRICK-CIRCLE:
>   Lay a brick,
>   turn right one degree,
>   move forward,
>   repeat three hundred sixty times.

> TOWER-CIRCLE (*how-high?*):
>   Make a BRICK-CIRCLE,
>   repeat *how-high* times.

"See? You make a circle of bricks, then put a circle on top of that, all the way to the top!"

"Ha ha ha, cute idea, girlie! But that can't possibly work."

"Why not?" said Laurie.

"It's too small!" Bruto said. "How do you expect to make a great big tower out of a teeny little plan like this?"

"I don't know," Laurie said. It seemed sensible to her, but maybe they knew something she didn't. They were professionals, after all. "I... I think it will work."

"Hmph," Bruto hmphed. "Even if it was big enough, it has a major flaw."

"What flaw?"

"Our first plan was a hollow square and fell down." Bruto said. "The second plan was a hollow square, twice as big, and it also fell down. Your plan is a hollow circle."

"I don't understand. Shouldn't a circle be stronger?"

"Obviously, the problem isn't shape or size, the problem is that they are *hollow inside*!" said Bruto. "We need to fill up the insides with brick, too. It's only logical."

"*You're right, Bruto!*" said one.

"*That's why you're the boss,*" said another.

"But I've seen hollow towers," said Laurie. "They've been built before."

"How do you know they won't fall down eventually? The evidence is very clear," said Bruto.

"*Yes, very clear,*" the other workers agreed, nodding to each other.

"But I—"

"No, I've made up my mind," Bruto said. "The tower must be solid. In fact," he said, looking at the pile, "We're going to build a pyramid."

"A pyramid?!"

"A pyramid can't fall down. It's already fallen down," explained Bruto. "It's one of the perfect solids!"

"*Yes, that's right!*"

"*Genius!*"

"*It's just a matter of more work and more materials.*"

"OK! We have a plan," said Bruto. "Everyone, let's get to work! Send Winsome my apologies, girlie, and tell her that we need more time to get it right."

Some people can't be argued with. As Laurie left, Bruto and his team were busy writing out the instructions for his PYRAMID, brick by brick by brick.

Chasing Elegants

"Right," said Winsome, ticking off an item on her list. "Elegant Island. Now where's that special package?"

"Wow, what kind of animals are those?" Along the shore, little grey animals with long grey trunks were playing with each other and napping in the sun.

"Those are the Elegants. The island is full of them."

"They're so small and graceful! It's like they're dancing."

"Yeah. Package, package..." Winsome muttered to herself. "Don't they have Elegants where you come from?"

"No. We have elephants but they are all big and clumsy. Are Elegants friendly?"

"Only as much as they need to be." Winsome said. "Found it! OK, this package is for Fresnel Goodglass."

"The address just says *UNDER THE RED BALLOON*," said Laurie. I guess that means he's over there." She pointed to a red globe floating above the trees.

But first, Laurie wanted to play with the Elegants. She approached them carefully, making soft *coo, coo* noises.

"Are you a bird now?" Xor snarked.

"*Shush. I'm just trying to get their attention.*"

The Elegants didn't seem especially scared or curious. In fact, they acted as though she wasn't there. But their dancing always seemed to take them out of her path. When she walked along the shore, the little creatures drifted inland. When she went inland, they decided that under the trees was the place to be. Soon she could see only a handful of Elegants, playing just outside of her reach. Oh, well.

With the balloon to guide them, finding the hill was easy enough. But when Laurie and Xor arrived there was nothing much there. A large boat anchor was half-buried in the earth. A rope led up, and up, and up to a basket way above the ground, which itself was attached to the balloon. A couple of young Elegants were playing hide-and-seek under the trees. There were no buildings or people at all.

"Are we in the right place?" she wondered. "Where is the lighthouse?"

"Hey Laurie, take a look at this." Xor was clinging to a sign that read *Please Ring for Service*. A little bell hung below it. They looked at each other and shrugged. Xor gave it a whack with his tail.

DONG-G-G-G-G-G-G-G-G-G-G-G-G-G-G

said the bell, much louder than such a tiny thing should be allowed to.
-G-G-G-G-G-G-G-G-G-G-G-G-G-G-G-G-G-G-G-G-G
Xor was right next to it. He turned bright indigo and fell to the ground.
-G-G-G-G-G-G-G-G-G-G-G-G-G-G-G-G-G-G-G-G-G-G-G-G
Laurie had to cover her ears until the sound died away.
-G-G-G-G-G-G-G-G-G-G-G-g-g-g...

When it was all over, the young Elegants were nowhere to be seen. She gathered the little lizard in her hands. His skin was white and his eyes were rolling round in different directions.

"Xor! Are you OK?"

"I think so. That scared the blue right out of me!"

A hissing sound from overhead made Laurie look up. An elevator box was lowering itself to the ground in front of them. They flinched as the door opened with a polite *ding!*

Laurie picked up her package, and with a last look around, stepped inside. The door closed shut and the elevator rose fast enough to make her toes crinkle and her stomach go roly-poly.

When the door opened again they were a hundred yards up in the air, inside the basket. It was like a little apartment. There was a desk, a bed, and some cozy chairs. A wrinkly-faced old man with a grey beard and pointy ears was smiling at her.

"Is this... are you Fresnel Goodglass? I'm Laurie. I have a package for you."

"Yes I am! Yes you are! And thank you!" he said, taking the package. "Welcome to my Floating Lighthouse. What do you think?"

"This isn't a *lighthouse*," Laurie said, testing the woven floor with her foot before getting off the elevator. "It's a balloon!"

"Sure it's a lighthouse. In balloon form. See the big light up there?" There was indeed a big lighthouse light hanging over them.

"But where's the long twisty staircase?" she asked.

"There is the elevator instead. Easier for my old bones."

"What about the watchman's room?"

"You can just look over the side of the basket."

"And the tower?"

"Don't need it! Inessential!" Fresnel said. "The essential part of a lighthouse is the *light*, not the house."

Laurie wasn't convinced. "You can't just stick a light on a balloon and call it a lighthouse."

"I can't?"

"No!"

"Why not?"

"Because... it's cheating," she said.

"Hmm. I think I see your point," Fresnel agreed. "But as long as it works, the name doesn't matter."

"Yes it does!"

"Maybe you're right," he agreed again. "But I am a terrible host! You must be thirsty after all that walking. Would you like some water?" Fresnel offered her a pitcher and glassware on a tray.

"Oh, yes, please." Laurie took a cup and tried to fill it. The water splashed onto her shoes.

"*Hey*! This cup has no bottom!"

"That's not a cup, dear child. It's a glass," he said.

"This *glass* has no bottom. How am I supposed to drink out of it?"

"On second thought, that's not properly a glass," said Fresnel. "It's a mug. See the handle?"

"Ok, this *mug* has—"

"On third thought," he said, stroking his beard, "it's made of glass, but also has a handle. So perhaps we should call it a glass-mug, or a mug-glass..."

"I don't care what you *call* it!" Laurie yelled. "It's *got no bottom* and the water... I mean, um, you called it a glass but it doesn't have... oh." She turned bright red.

Fresnel handed Laurie another mug-glass-cup. "You're right again. Things are what they are, no matter what names people give them."

"But aren't names important?" Laurie asked, checking the bottom of her new glass-cup-mug carefully.

"Names go only so far. And many names are actually the same thing in disguise."

"Really?"

"Surely. Are you Laurie or Lauren?"

"When mom is really mad, she calls me Lauren." She put her hands on her hips and threw her head back. "*Lauren Ipsum, come downstairs NOW!*"

Fresnel laughed like a horse would laugh, if the horse had heard the joke. "A full name is a powerful thing. But you're the same person either way. And sometimes different things have the same name. You call your mom 'mom', but I call my mom 'mom' too."

"But I wouldn't call *your* mom 'mom'!" said Laurie. *How weird would that be?*

"There you go. It's only logical. You have to look *past* the name to see things as they really are. That's Fresnel's First Law."

"You sound just like Eponymous Bach."

"Really? Well, I'm a Composer too," said Fresnel. "I start with big ideas and make them smaller."

"Make them smaller? Why?"

"Why not? Only people with small minds think Big Problems need Big Ideas."

Laurie wasn't sure what he was talking about. "How do you make an idea smaller?"

"By *De*composing. How would you talk about a lighthouse without using the word 'lighthouse'?"

"Well, it's a tall white tower near the sea, with a room full of windows at the top, and a big light on top of that, and a long twisty staircase inside."

"That's very good," Fresnel said. "Now look at each part and see if it's essential. If your tall-tower-by-the-sea-with-windows-and-big-light-and-staircase was *pink*, would it work just the same?"

"I guess so. I've never seen a pink lighthouse." she said.

"Neither have I! But if everything already existed, life would be pretty boring. Why is your lighthouse tall?"

"So boats can see you," said Laurie. "A short lighthouse wouldn't work so well. And you need the twisty staircase to get to the top."

"Why the light?"

"The light is so they can see you at night."

"And the watchman's room?"

"So you can see *them*."

"Ah, so," said Fresnel. "My balloon has a light very high up so people far away can see it. I can look over the side and see them. I get to the top by elevator. The color doesn't matter. It does everything a lighthouse does. Is it a lighthouse?"

"It's *like* a lighthouse," she admitted.

"You drive a hard bargain! I'll settle for 'like a lighthouse'," he said.

"So that's how you decompose?"

"That's it, more or less. You take a big idea apart, and see the why behind each part. Then you look for smaller ideas that do the same thing. For instance, what did you think of my little bell?"

"Your little *bell*! That thing frightened the b—"

"It needs some adjustments, I agree. But the idea is sound," he said. "The essential part of a bell is the sound. Because the bell is way down on the ground it needs a big sound so I can hear it."

"So why don't you use a big bell, then?" she asked.

"If I used a big bell I'd need a big frame to hang it from, and a big ringer, and a big sign to go along with it all. All the inessentials get bigger," Fresnel said. "There's no need to use a big, complex idea when a small simple one will do."

"I wish I could tell Bruto that," Laurie said, remembering his giant pyramid. "But he's so far away."

———

"Winsome, why am I delivering so many telescopes?"

114

Winsome's expression turned stony. "It's not nice to open other people's mail."

"I'm sorry. Those packages are really heavy and I wondered what could be so fragile and expensive and important..."

Winsome didn't say anything. She pretended to be busy with ropes and anchors and winches.

Laurie pressed again. "Why telescopes?"

"The telescopes are so the lighthouse keepers can see farther out."

"Why do they need to see farther out?"

"Because the other lighthouses are too far away."

"That doesn't make any sense," Laurie said. "Why do people in lighthouses want to see other lighthouses?"

"Because it's how we're going to send messages. It's the Lighthouse Network."

"Why do you want to send messages that way?"

"Right now," said Winsome, "if someone on Abstract Island wants to talk with someone else on Data Island, they have to pay the Colonel and his Network of mail daemons."

"Is that a bad thing? Why build your own Network?"

"Because I can. And because Colonel Trapp doesn't want me to."

"Why doesn't he want you to build a Network?"

"That's Five Whys already, kiddo. Are you ready to go? The next stop is an easy one. You'll like Ping. She lives in a treehouse!"

Many Hands Make Light Work

A young woman was waiting for Laurie at the base of an enormous tree. A long twisty staircase wrapped around the trunk and up into the leaves.

"Hello, Laurie! Glad you made it. My name is Ping Baudot. I've been waiting for you."

"Hello. Wait, how did you know my name?"

"Oh, Fresnel told me all about you."

"Fresnel? He lives way over on Elegant Island!"

"Yes, isn't it wonderful? You and Winsome have been making lots of deliveries lately. The Network is getting quite big now! I can hardly keep up with all the chatter."

"But I don't—"

"You should be very proud. Here, let me help you with that." Ping took the package and raced up the stairs, round and round the trunk of the tree. Laurie followed as best she could. When they arrived at the treehouse near the top, she gasped in surprise. It was a *treelighthouse*! Not only that, the watchman's room was filled with telescopes pointing in all directions. Neat labels were attached to each one.

"Well? What do you think?" Ping said.

"Why do you need so many telescopes?"

"See for yourself."

Laurie put an eye to the 'scope labeled ELEGANT. A red round splotch was hanging in the air. And was that a rope...?

"Hey, that's Fresnel's balloon! I can see him! He's waving!"

Laurie looked into other telescopes. Each one was pointed at a different lighthouse. The one for ABSTRACT showed the lighthouse keeper who didn't say very much, up in his tall white tower by the sea, looking back through a telescope of his own. He didn't wave. The BYZANTIUM telescope showed half a pyramid covered in giant mechanical turtles. Bruto was busy counting bricks.

Ping put down the heavy package Laurie had delivered and released the latches. Inside was a squat telescope. "We use the telescopes to be able to see each other."

"Why do you all want to see each other? What are all these telescopes *for*?"

"For the Network," Ping said. "It's how we pass messages. Watch this." She went to the middle of the room and turned a giant wheel until a red arrow pointed directly at Elegant Island. Then she pulled a lever up and down quickly:

FLOP. FLOP. FLIP. FLOP. FLIP.
FLOP. FLIP. FLIP. FLOP. FLOP.

"Now look at Fresnel again," she said.

Laurie put an eye to his telescope. Fresnel had pointed *his* light at *them* and began blinking a message:

FLOOSH. FLOOSH. FLASH. FLOOSH. FLASH.
FLOOSH. FLASH. FLASH. FLOOSH. FLOOSH.

"He answered back! What did he say?"

"Oh, he just said 'hi'."

"All that just for 'hi'?"

"That's how the Baudot Code works. Sentences are made of words, and words are made of letters, right? In the same way, we make *letters* out of FLIPs and FLOPs. Like this:"

```
01001 = L
11000 = A
10011 = U
01010 = R
01100 = I
10000 = E
```

"That's pretty neat! But I still think it's a lot of work just to say 'hi'."

"Maybe you're right," Ping said, smiling. "But now that the hard work of building the Network is finished, we can do something *really* interesting: use the Network to make itself better."

"How do you do that?"

"Well, I'm working on a way to use two colors of lights. Fresnel has an idea for a simpler Code that uses only four FLIPs or FLOPs, though I'm not too sure how that will work. We use the old Baudot Code to talk to each other about our ideas for new codes, and then try them out."

"Oh, I see! You can use the Network to talk about how to use the Network."

"And you helped do it, Laurie, by delivering all of those telescopes. Now the Network will only get better and better as we learn how to use it. We can already pass a message from one end of the Network to the other in just a few minutes! Even the *Doppelganger* takes a couple of days to deliver the mail that far. Everyone will want to use it once we work out the bugs."

"But... what about Winsome? Is she going to lose her job?"

"What? No, not at all! The Network was her idea."

"It was?"

"Sure! All of us work for Winsome. She doesn't want to spend her days hauling mail bags around. That reminds me," Ping said, searching through a pile of paper, "Winsome says she has one more job for you."

"Oh. What is it?"

"She wants you to deliver this letter to a person on the other side of the Garden of the Forking Paths."

There was no name on the envelope, but this wasn't half as strange as some of the assignments Laurie had been given. If she got it done quickly she could come back here and play with the Network. "So where is the Garden?"

"You're in a hurry, huh? I'll show you where it is."

Branching Out

The Garden was surrounded by a hedge at least eight feet tall. The entrance was an archway cut out of the bushes. A wooden sign above the entrance said

WELCOME TO THE GARDEN
OF THE FORKING PATHS.

"Here we go," said Ping.

Laurie was suddenly very worried. "Ping, is this a laba... laber... one of those garden mazes?" Laurie had read stories about little girls and garden mazes, and they never ended well. Garden mazes were full of Monsters and twisty little passages between you and the exit.

"It's not really a labyrinth. You can always find a way out," said Ping. "Where you end up is a different story."

"Oh, good. After I deliver this letter, can I come back to the Tree-lighthouse? Maybe we can ask the Network about how to find Hamilton!"

"That's... a good idea. Yes. When you're done, if you want, we can talk about it."

"Thank you! See you soon!"

"Goodbye, Laurie. Take care of yourself."

She stepped through the entrance into a kind of hallway made of more bushes. After a short walk she found a small fountain with a sign above it.

LEAVE A COIN. MAKE A WISH.

Laurie dropped her last Fair Coin into the fountain, closed her eyes, and made a wish. She held her eyes closed for an extra moment just in case. Anyway, nothing exciting happened.

She kept walking down the green hallway. There wasn't much to see except hedges, and more hedges, and more signs that talked about the Garden.

DID YOU KNOW?
THERE ARE 16,777,216 PATHS
THROUGH THE GARDEN.

"Only sixteen million? That's nothing!" she said. "Userland had millions of millions of *millions*."

ONLY ONE PATH PER VISITOR.

"That's OK. I want to get through here quickly."

ONLY ONE VISITOR PER PATH.

"Isn't that the same thing?"

NO.

"I wonder which path is the shortest," she said. The next sign answered her question.

ALL PATHS ARE THE SAME LENGTH.

"Then how do I know which one to take?" she said.

CHOOSE WISELY.

That's when she came to the first fork in the path. Each fork had its own sign. The lefthand sign said

⇐ THINGS.

121

And the righthand sign said

IDEAS. ⇒

Laurie had seen a lot of Ideas lately. A simple Thing would be a nice change. She took the lefthand path. A minute later she came to the next fork. The signs there said

⇐ FAMILIAR THINGS.
STRANGE THINGS. ⇒

"I've seen a lot of Strange Things lately, too," she said. "I'll go for Familiar."

⇐ YOUNG.   OLD. ⇒

"Um... Old!" Down the righthand path.

⇐ INTERESTING.
BORING. ⇒

"That's an easy one," said Xor. "Interesting."

"You're not the one who has to climb rocks and cross scary bridges when we make Interesting deliveries," Lauie said. "But, OK."

⇐ LOST.
UNLOST. ⇒

"How can you have a sign pointing to Lost things? Wouldn't that make them Unlost?"

"Maybe they are only Lost until you find them."

"That makes sense." They took the left path.

⇐ MOSTLY LOST.

COMPLETELY LOST. ⇒

"Comp... no, *Mostly* Lost." Leftward again.

"You know, I don't see any millions of paths," said Xor. "There's only ever two."

⇐ SMALL.

NOT-SMALL. ⇒

"Not-Small!" they said together.

BIGGER THAN YOU?

⇐ NO.   YES. ⇒

"Everything is bigger than me," said Xor. "Let's go right."

BIGGER THAN A MOUNTAIN?

⇐ YES.   NO. ⇒

Not that big! They went right again.

TALLER THAN A LIGHTHOUSE?

⇐ NO.   YES. ⇒

Laurie had seen quite enough of lighthouses too, thank you. She tried to go left but a Shelled Green Round animal barred the way.

"We meet again, Miss Ipsum," it said.

"*Mister Tortoise!* What are you doing here?"

"I'm enjoying a special treat," said Tortoise, taking a bite out of the greenery. "I help keep the mandelbroccoli bushes in the Garden nice and trim. For me it is a delicious chore. And what are you doing here, Miss Ipsum?"

"I'm looking for the nearest exit so I can deliver a letter."

Tortoise seemed to smile. Of course, he always seemed to be smiling. "There are millions of paths through the Garden. All of them are exactly the same length."

She tried to picture so many paths side by side. "I don't understand. If there are so many, where are they?"

"They are all around you. Every path forks off from another path," Tortoise said. "One path becomes two, becomes four, eight, sixteen, and so on. After twenty-four forkings there are over sixteen million different paths."

"Oh! It's the Power of Two again. But this time it gets bigger instead of smaller."

"Exactly right. You are currently on the path to Things that are Familiar, Old, Interesting, Mostly Lost, Bigger Than You and Smaller Than A Mountain," said Tortoise. "I suppose I am one of them."

"So how do I choose which forks to take?"

"I suggest choosing wisely. Good day, Miss Ipsum." Tortoise turned and walked slowly and steadily down the lefthand path.

"Wait! I don't know what you mean!" Laurie ran after him. Catching up with a Tortoise should have been easy. But with every step he got farther and farther away. By the time she got to the next fork he was nowhere to be seen.

⇐ FRIENDLY.

UNFRIENDLY. ⇒

"What do you think, Xor? Which way?"

"Do you really want to see a Garden full of Unfriendly Things?"

"Good point." She went left.

⇐ IN THE AIR.

ON THE GROUND. ⇒

They didn't want to see anything bigger than them that also could fly, no matter how Friendly. Anyway, Tortoise was on the ground.

⇐ LIGHT.

HEAVY. ⇒

"Heavy!"

⇐ LIVES OUTSIDE.

LIVES INSIDE. ⇒

"Tortoises live outside, don't they?"

⇐ NEVER SLEEPS.

SOMETIMES SLEEPS.⇒

"And they definitely sleep," said Xor. Rightward.

⇐ SLEEPS AT NIGHT.

SLEEPS DURING THE DAY.⇒

"Sleeps at Night! We should be getting close!"

⇐ MANY COLORS.

ONE COLOR. ⇒

Laurie ran down the lefthand path without stopping to think. But wasn't Tortoise only one color? It was too late to go back.

125

⇐ QUIET.
NOISY. ⇒

"I don't like Noisy Things," she said. "Tortoise is pretty quiet."

⇐ PLURAL.
SINGULAR. ⇒

"What does that mean?"

"Plural means more than one. Singular means only one," Xor said. They went right.

⇐ NATIVE.
FOREIGN. ⇒

"I know this one," said Laurie. "Native means from here. Foreign means from somewhere else."

⇐ EXPECTED.
UNEXPECTED. ⇒

"I wonder where we are going to end up," she said. "What is Familiar, Old, Interesting, Mostly Lost, Bigger Than Me but Shorter Than A Lighthouse, Friendly, On The Ground, Heavy, that Lives Outside, Sleeps At Night—" (she paused to breathe) "—has Many Colors, is Quiet, Singular, Native, *and* Unexpected?"

⇐ YOUR WISH.
SOMEONE ELSE'S WISH. ⇒

"MY wish!" said Xor and Laurie at the same time. They giggled and walked down the left path. The next sign made them think for a moment. It said

126

ARE YOU SURE?
⇐ YES.   NO. ⇒

"Sure I'm sure!" said Laurie. "Why would I ever want someone else's wish?" She went down the lefthand path. "I think we're almost through the Garden, Xor!"

She started walking fast, then jogging, then running again down the long green hallway. Xor was getting excited too, turning all sorts of polka-dot colors. She was already thinking about what messages she wanted to send to Fresnel, and Tinker, and—

"Oh no!"

Laurie stopped dead in her tracks. In front of them was another forking. The last one.

The lefthand sign said

⇐ HAMILTON.

And the righthand sign said

VANA. ⇒

"The Garden guessed my wish!" Laurie said.

"Yeah. Mine too." Xor said.

Laurie started to go left, then stopped. Then she started to go right, but had second thoughts. They stood there for a very long and very silent minute.

"We can only take one path," she said.

"Yeah," he said.

"And there's no going back."

"That's the rule."

"You really want to find your aunt."

"You really want to go back home."

"That means we have to choose," Laurie said. "But how?" She did want to go home, but she also wanted Xor to find Vana. She wanted to bring Xor and Vana home with her and how cool would that be and—

"No, Laurie." Xor said sadly. "It means we have to split up."

"But—"

"Only One Visitor Per Path. That's the rule." He jumped off her shoulder and landed on the righthand sign. "I guess... this is how you found me." His skin turned orange and purple.

"We can do this," said Laurie, thinking furiously. "Once you find your Aunt Vana, take her to the Treelighthouse. I'll find a way to come back. Or maybe I'll get a telescope and a big light and—"

"We'll see each other again," Xor said.

"OK," said Laurie. "Promise?"

"Promise."

"And I'm going to whistle, OK?"

"OK."

"So you can hear me."

"Right."

"It'll be fine."

"Absolutely."

"Here I go."

"Me too."

Laurie did try to whistle, but it's impossible to whistle and cry at the same time. Just try it.

Fin

The mandelbroccoli bushes got shorter and wilder until they blended in with the forest. Laurie didn't know where she was or where she was going. But she knew how to get there. At least she hoped she did. By then it was late afternoon and the shadows were getting longer.

The trees of the forest were large oaks and maple, with an occasional pine or spruce. There were a number of saplings and bushes of various sorts. It was hard to see far because of all the leaves, but walking was easy enough if she skirted round the spruce and berry bushes.

"*Chirrrup!*"

Laurie's heart started pounding. More Jargon? How many? Where?

"*Chirrrup!*"

No running this time. She walked towards the noise as quietly as she could. It seemed to be behind a large tree. No, not a Jargon. It was... a squirrel. An ordinary squirrel. It yelled what were probably very nasty things in Squirrel then ran up the tree to safety. And that tree! She recognized it. It was the big tree behind her house, at the edge of the woods...

Laurie was home.

———

Lying in her own bed after a hot bath made Laurie feel happy and tired. As far as her mother knew, Laurie had been gone only for an hour or two. It felt like at least a week since she'd gotten lost in the woods. She was too sleepy to think about it. She hoped Xor had found his wish and was learning how to blend in. She was sad that she didn't get to see her new friends again. She had promised to come back... after delivering... delivering that letter...

Two seconds later she was out of bed and tearing open the plain white envelope.

Hi, kiddo. If you're reading this letter you've figured out who it was for. I wasn't sure the Garden would actually work, and I don't like goodbyes.

You helped us build the Network. We couldn't have done it without you. Fresnel says once you learn a few things & un-learn some others, you'll make a good Composer.

See you around,
Capt. Winsome "Losesome" Trapp

She read it twice before she noticed that Winsome's real name was Trapp. It made sense. For all of the sour things Winsome said about Colonel Trapp, they were a lot alike, sending strange messages and bossing people around. It looked like Laurie wasn't the only one who had trouble getting along with her parents.

She lay down again and thought about tomorrow. Tomorrow was the first day of summer school. It didn't sound as scary as it did be-fore. If she could navigate the Byzantine Process, beat Ponens and Tol-lens, make infinite strings, and teach turtles to build towers, sitting in a classroom didn't sound that hard at all.

She might even learn something interesting.

The End

One More Thing

It was a dark and foggy night, many months after Lauren Ipsum had gone back home to Hamilton. A lighthouse flashed. Flashed. Flashed. Flashed.

The flashes didn't carry any messages this night. The fog was too thick to send signals, and so the Network was down. Anyway, the powerful lights were needed for their original purpose: to warn boats away from dangerous rocks.

As it happened, only one boat was around, and it didn't need warning. It was exactly where it was supposed to be.

The *Cheeky Tulip* was the boat, and Kevin Kelvin was her captain. It was large and flat and plain. Near the front was a little cabin where Kelvin lived. The rest of the deck was taken up by a winch and crane. A wire led from the crane and into the water, looking for all the world like a large fishing pole. Belowdecks was mostly a hold for tons and tons of coiled wire.

It wouldn't be accurate to say that the *Tulip* was a gigantic boat with a winch attached to it. That might give you the wrong impression. It would be better to describe it as a gigantic *winch* with a boat attached to it. Its entire purpose in life was to play out and wind up miles of heavy wire.

Inside the cabin, Kevin Kelvin rubbed his hands together to keep them warm. A thermometer hung from a peg near the door. It read a chilly 273 degrees. *Brrrrr!*

273 degrees might sound pretty hot to you and me, but this was on the Kelvin Scale, one of his many inventions. The Kelvin Scale starts at Absolute Zero, the coldest that any cold thing can possibly get. Zero degrees Kelvin is cold enough to *freeze time*. 273 degrees Kelvin isn't much better. It's about the temperature of an ice cube. *Brrrrr!*

The thermometer said a lot about the kind of person Kevin Kelvin was. He was a Composer, and a wickedly smart one. He never let a good idea escape without his name on it.

When people asked Kelvin what he was doing he would say he was fishing. He never explained what he was fishing *for*, in the middle of the night with a gigantic winch that had a boat attached to it. When people made jokes about catching sea monsters, Kelvin only smiled. No one knew what he knew. How could they?

Kevin Kelvin was fishing for tiny, tiny bits of electricity flowing up his Wire. The Wire traveled under the ocean for miles, all the way to a little building on the shore, not far from the lighthouse. He twiddled dials, and listened carefully, and made notes. If his ideas were right, any moment now, he should hear a signal from his assistant on the other end. It would sound like—

BEEP.

His skin tingled with excitement, but he didn't dare make a sound.

BLOOP. BEEP.

Kelvin quickly disconnected some wires and connected some other ones. He flicked a switch on and off.

FLIP. FLOP. FLIP.

The wire answered back.

BLOOP.

Just as he thought. The Wire worked. Under miles of seawater, it worked. If the *Tulip* laid down a Wire all the way between two islands, that would form the first link in Kelvin's very own Network. A Network that could send messages all the time, even on a terrible night like this. A Network that, someday, could even have *multiple Wires*.

Those fools up there in their ivory towers, flashing their little lights, will never know what hit them!

Notes

A few readers have wondered whether this or that part of the story is real. Can you really make a Fair Coin out of an Unfair Coin? Can you really use ants to find shorter paths? Yes you can — and a lot more besides.

Achilles and the Tortoise: These two characters were used by Zeno of Elea almost 2,500 years ago to talk about interesting wrinkles of infinity. From Aristotle to Lewis Carroll to Marvin Minsky to Douglas Hofstadter, mathematics is full of stories about their adventures. It's Tortoises all the way down.

Algorithm: is another way to say "how to do something". A recipe for how to make pizza is an algorithm. So is a recipe for how to figure out the answer to a problem. Things get really interesting when you think about algorithms for algorithms, that is to say, how to figure out how to figure out how to do something. See also *Infinite Regress*.

Ampere: André-Marie Ampère worked out how electricity flowing through parallel wires will make them either attract or repel each other. Ampère used this idea to lay the foundations of everything we know about electricity. Thus the world was left tragically paperclipless until they were finally invented in 1867. Our measure of electrical current is called an "ampere" or "amp" in his honor. See *Bach's Third Law*.

Ants: are very good at finding short paths between food and the nest, even though they are mostly blind. Their trick is to take random routes, and lay down a scent for others to follow. Because the scent fades over time, a shorter path will have a stronger scent trail. Eventually they converge on the shortest one.

Real ants can't solve the Wandering Salesman problem, because as soon as they find a bit of food they turn around and go right back home. But virtual ants, which are programmed to go to the next town instead, do quite well.

Bach's Third Law of Eponymy: As a thing becomes more useful and famous, its name becomes shorter and lowercase. This law was first noted by Richard Hamming, the inventor of "hamming codes". Spelled with a little h.

Baudot: In 1870 Émile Baudot invented one of the first codes for digital communication, naturally named after himself. Better codes eventually replaced the Baudot Code, but his name lives on (shorter and lowercase) as the "baud", a measure of how many symbols are transmitted per second.

Bruto Fuerza: thinks the answer to every problem is more power and brute force. If you make your building twice as tall, twice as wide and twice as thick, it will be eight times heavier because you are doubling the mass in all three dimensions. But it will only be *four* times as strong, because strength is measured in *two* dimensions.

In his own way Bruto is right. If you pile on enough bricks, you'll eventually make a pyramid tall enough to be a lighthouse. But his kind of thinking has enormous costs. When your algorithm collapses, a smart thing to do is to change your point of view, not pile on more bricks. See *Five Whys*.

Chasing Your Tail: is not always a waste of time. See also *Recursion*.

Circle: The turtle game Laurie plays in the shop of N. Veterate Tinker is based on research carried out by Alan Kay and Seymour Papert. Ten-year-olds often discover the CIRCLE algorithm. *Five*-year-olds often discover a more efficient algorithm, MOTH-CIRCLE.

So here's an interesting question: what number should you plug in to MOTH-CIRCLE in order to draw a circle two inches in diameter?

Composing: Fresnel, Tinker, and Eponymous all talk about three basic ways to play with ideas: Composing, Relating, and Decomposing. These three methods are at the root of all math, logic, and computer science.

Composing is combining little ideas into big ones. Laurie's idea for drawing a circle is composed of the simpler ideas of turning, moving, making a mark, and repeating. Almost every idea is composed of other ideas. For example, multiplying whole numbers isn't anything special. It can be thought of as adding and repeating:

$2 \times 3 = 6$

$2 + 2 + 2 = 6$ (Add two, repeat three times.)

Decomposing starts with a big idea and takes it apart. A good way to take an idea apart is to describe it without using its name.

Even simple ideas like 3 and 4 can be decomposed into even simpler ideas. Start with zero, then add one. Then add one, and add one, and so on:

$0 = 0$

$1 = 0 + 1$

$2 = 0 + 1 + 1$

$3 = 0 + 1 + 1 + 1$

$4 = 0 + 1 + 1 + 1 + 1$

...etc, etc, and so forth.

If you really wanted to, you could just use zero and one and ditch all the other numbers. I don't recommend it —you'll use up a lot of paper!— but it's a perfectly valid way to do math.

$2 + 2 = 4$

$(0 + 1 + 1) + (0 + 1 + 1) = (0 + 1 + 1 + 1 + 1)$

Doppelganger: If you replace all of the parts of a boat, do you still have the same boat? If you reassemble the old parts, which boat is the original? What if you only replaced half of the parts?

Fair Coin: There is no such thing as a perfectly fair coin, but nearly all coins are fair enough, especially if you flip them instead of spinning them on a table. Even so, for important things like physics simulations, or choosing who gets to ride in the front seat, flipping twice guarantees absolute fairness. Trent's algorithm was first described by John von Neumann in 1951.

Trent actually gives Laurie a pretty good deal, trading only two of her coins for one Fair Coin. At least half the time you'll get an HH or TT and start over. That means on average you'll need at least three coin flips for each Fair flip.

Five Whys: also known as root cause analysis. You keep asking Why questions until you find out Where things went Wrong. There are a lot of mental games to help you avoid or learn from mistakes. Another good one is "Never worry alone".

Fresnel: Augustin-Jean Fresnel was a real person who invented a way of focusing big lighthouse lights with only a little bit of glass. His idea was that lenses didn't have to be big and thick to do the job. The essential part of a lens is how different angles of the surface bend light. So instead of one huge piece of glass, the Fresnel lens is an arrangement of small pieces of glass at different angles. They are still used in lighthouses today.

Gliders: are part of a wondrous thing called Conway's Game of Life. If you've never heard of it, you are in for a beautiful surprise.

Hamiltonian Path: visits every town on a map exactly once. In the book I use the word path, but there is a slight difference between a hamiltonian path and a hamiltonian *cycle*, which is a path that returns to where it started. William Hamilton was a mathematician, and mathematicians are fussy people who are very precise about what words mean.

On a map with N towns, there are $(N-1)! \div 2$ cycles. Finding a cycle is fairly easy because there are so many of them. Finding a *short* one is the hard part. See also *Wandering Salesman*.

Hugh Rustic: embodies the idea of a "heuristic", a way to find Good Enough answers to very hard problems. These are most often used with combinatorial problems, where there are many many many possible answers and no efficient way to find which one is the best.

Garden of the Forking Paths: At each fork Laurie answered an either/or question that cut the number of possible paths in half. The same principle is used in the game Twenty Questions: if you choose your questions (or answers) carefully, you can arrive at virtually anything in only 20 or 30 steps. See also *Recursion*.

Infinity: You might imagine that "infinity" contains everything you can possibly think of, plus everything you can't. But that's not quite true. There are infinite *kinds* of infinity, and infinite roads to them.

There is an infinity of odd numbers: 1, 3, 5, 7, 9... up to forever. There is also an infinity of even numbers: 0, 2, 4, 6, 8, etc, etc, and so forth. But no matter how hard you look, you will never find an odd number on the list of even numbers, or an even number among the odd ones.

Infinite Regress: If you think about how you think, you might then start thinking about how you think about how you think, and then about how you think about how you think about how you think, etc. The first time you fall into this mental trap it can be confusing or even scary. The trick is not to take it too seriously. See also *Chasing Your Tail*.

Improbable: not as hard as impossible.

Impossible: harder than improbable.

It's Only Logical: being logical isn't the same as being true. It's easy for an idea to be simple, logical and *false*, because there is something you forgot to consider. It's also easy for logic to get stuck in endless loops. See *Ponens* and *Infinite Regress*.

Jane Hecate: checks each letter of Laurie's guesses one by one until there is a mismatch with the password. So a guess that is mostly correct will take longer to fail, so Laurie knows how warm or cold she is. This is called a *timing attack*. Many people who should know better make Jane's mistake, and leak information about the secret they are keeping.

Jargon: In the real world, a Jargon doesn't look like a mouse-dog, or even a dog-mouse. It looks just like an ordinary word. Jargon can be silly, or powerful, or dangerous, depending on how you use it. But if you always obfuscate instead of explicate, no one will understand you!

Kelvin: Lord Kelvin was a real person who composed a large number of clever algorithms while helping to build the first telegraph Network. He also figured out that there was such a thing as Absolute Zero. Using the money he made from the Network, Kelvin bought a boat. He sailed around the world, laying more cables, writing more algorithms, and putting his name on them. The story of Kelvin and the telegraph Network is a very interesting one, but also a very long one. Perhaps it's better to leave it for another time.

Mandelbroccoli: does exist, and it's the weirdest-looking vegetable I know. At the market it's called "Romanesco".

Laurie's algorithm for moving the wolf, the goat, and mandelbroccoli uses what's called a *counting argument*. You can solve some problems by ignoring unimportant differences between things, and only counting how many there are. Another trick is to count different ways to see if they add up.

- Reader or writer, only one can use a book at a time.
- Mandelbroc or wolf, don't leave the goat alone with it.
- Count the gaps *between* the posts and you get ten. Count the posts and you get eleven.

When Tinker tells Laurie to ignore paths that are mirror images of other paths, like BCD and DCB, and count them as one, he is using a counting argument. This cuts the number of paths through Userland in half. But even cutting the number in half doesn't help much with the Salesman Problem. A Very Big Number divided by a small number is still a Very Big Number.

Poem: Writing an algorithm should be just as easy as writing a simple poem. It's not that easy yet, but it's gotten better. One of the jobs of Composers is to figure out ways to make it simpler and easier to describe their algorithms.

Ponens: a type of logical argument. His full name is Modus Podendo Ponens. For example:

- If only people with passwords can enter,
  then our door is secure

- Only people with passwords have entered

- Therefore, our door is secure

While this may sound simple and obvious and logical, it's not necessarily true. Logic is only as good as the assumptions it depends on. If the person who *says* she is Eponymous Bach is not actually Eponymous Bach, all of the logic in the world won't help you. See also *Tollens*.

Recursion: Recursion is a very deep and useful idea. Say Jane Hecate wants a faster way to find the name "Lauren" in her book of names. She can divide the book into two equal halves and see if L is in the first half or the second half. She then divides the first half of the book into quarters, then eighths, and so on. This quickly narrows her search to the right page.

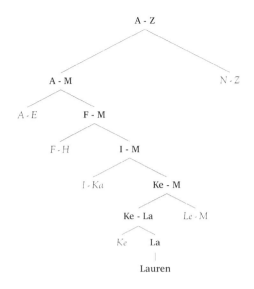

That's recursion: you run though the steps of an algorithm, and if the answer is the one you want, you stop. If it's not, you take the answer, plug it into the algorithm, and run it again. See also *Garden of Forking Paths* and *Chasing Your Tail*.

Relating: is putting two ideas side-by-side and comparing, like Fresnel's balloon and a lighthouse. With numbers you use the < sign to show that the number on the left is smaller than the one on the right. You use the = sign to show that the stuff on the left is equal to the stuff on the right.

$2 < 3$

$2 \times 3 = 6$

There are fuzzier relations, too. Fresnel's balloon isn't exactly a lighthouse, but it's kind of sort of almost like a lighthouse:

(elevator, balloon, light) *is-like-a* (staircase, tower, light)

Sense: you say an algorithm makes sense when you think it will actually work. But that doesn't mean it makes sense for *your* problem, or that it is sensible.

Sensible: an algorithm is sensible if it works, and works quickly.

Steganosaurus: steganography is the art of hiding information inside other information. A Steganosaurus is, therefore, a dinosaur that can hide itself anywhere. No one has ever actually seen a Steganosaurus, but that doesn't prove anything. See also *Tollens*.

Tollens: is a logical argument. He's kind of like Ponens, but backwards:

- If Steganosauruses existed, you would see them.
- You have never seen a Steganosaurus.
- Therefore, they do not exist.

Like Ponens, Modus Tollendo Tollens is perfectly valid logic. But it's only as good as the assumptions used to make it. The absence of proof is not always proof of absence. Maybe they live on an island you've never been to. Or maybe they are so good at hiding no one can see them. See *It's Only Logical*.

Wandering Salesman: Not all who wander are lost. He uses a heuristic algorithm, called nearest-neighbor, to find a short hamiltonian cycle through all the towns. It works except when it doesn't. A very interesting thing about the Salesman Problem is that humans are pretty good at solving small examples by hand. There is much discussion about what algorithm people use in their heads while solving it.

Something to think about: is Hugh Rustic's ant-map through Userland the shortest possible path? Or is it only a short-enough path? Can you do better?

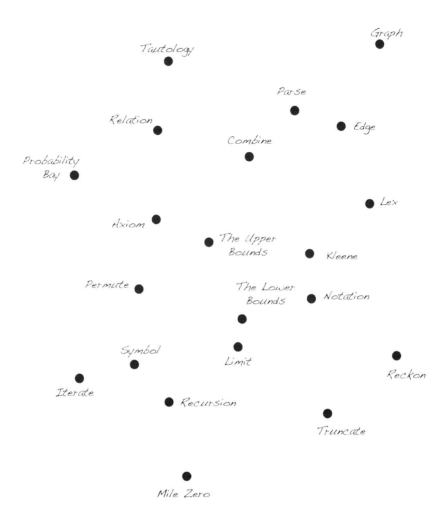

Graph

Tautology

Parse

Relation   Edge

Combine

Probability
Bay   Lex

Axiom

The Upper
Bounds   Kleene

Permute
                    The Lower
                    Bounds   Notation

Symbol   Reckon

                    Limit

Iterate

        Recursion

                    Truncate

Mile Zero

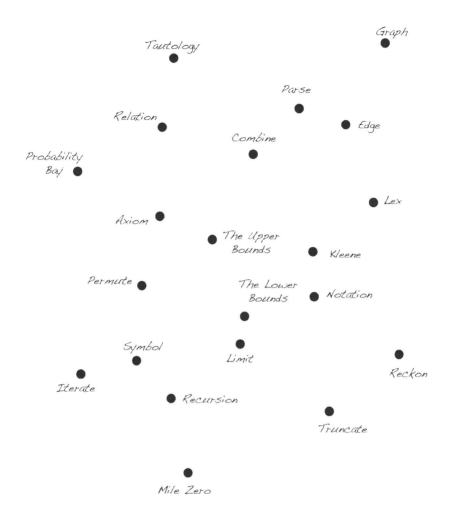

Graph

Tautology

Parse

Relation

Edge

Combine

Probability
Bay

Lex

Axiom

The Upper
Bounds

Kleene

Permute

The Lower
Bounds

Notation

Symbol

Limit

Reckon

Iterate

Recursion

Truncate

Mile Zero

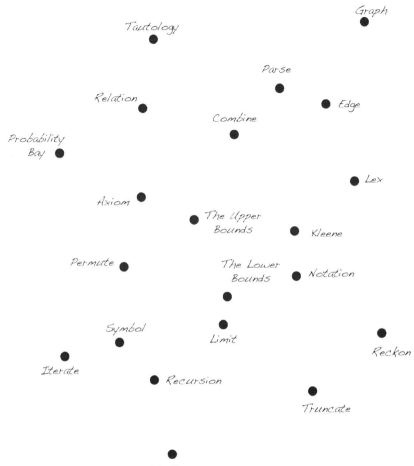

Graph

Tautology

Parse

Relation   Edge

Combine

Probability
Bay

Lex

Axiom

The Upper
Bounds   Kleene

Permute

The Lower
Bounds   Notation

Symbol
Limit

Reckon

Iterate

Recursion

Truncate

Mile Zero

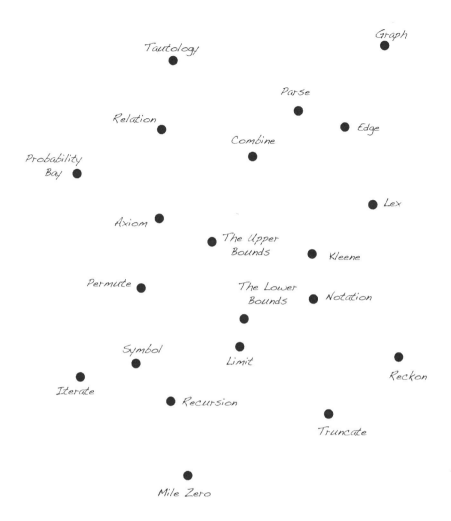

Graph

Tautology

Parse

Relation

Edge

Combine

Probability
Bay

Lex

Axiom

The Upper
Bounds

Kleene

Permute

The Lower
Bounds

Notation

Symbol

Limit

Reckon

Iterate

Recursion

Truncate

Mile Zero